SETH PATRICK

Cryptid: The Mothman's Apprentice

First published by Boyd Hill House 2025

Copyright © 2025 by Seth Patrick

All rights reserved. No part of this publication may be reproduced, stored or transmitted in any form or by any means, electronic, mechanical, photocopying, recording, scanning, or otherwise without written permission from the publisher. It is illegal to copy this book, post it to a website, or distribute it by any other means without permission.

This novel is entirely a work of fiction. The names, characters and incidents portrayed in it are the work of the author's imagination. Any resemblance to actual persons, living or dead, events or localities is entirely coincidental.

Seth Patrick asserts the moral right to be identified as the author of this work.

Seth Patrick has no responsibility for the persistence or accuracy of URLs for external or third-party Internet Websites referred to in this publication and does not guarantee that any content on such Websites is, or will remain, accurate or appropriate.

Designations used by companies to distinguish their products are often claimed as trademarks. All brand names and product names used in this book and on its cover are trade names, service marks, trademarks and registered trademarks of their respective owners. The publishers and the book are not associated with any product or vendor mentioned in this book. None of the companies referenced within the book have endorsed the book.

First edition

ISBN: 979-8-9921921-0-0

Cover art by Roderick Brydon

*This book was professionally typeset on Reedsy.
Find out more at reedsy.com*

For the kid who watched too much TV

"If I speak in the tongues of men or of angels, but do not have love, I am only a resounding gong or a clanging cymbal."

1 Corinthians 13:1 NIV

Contents

1	Chapter 1	1
2	Chapter 2	8
3	Chapter 3	19
4	Chapter 4	27
5	Chapter 5	38
6	Chapter 6	44
7	Chapter 7	53
8	Chapter 8	58
9	Chapter 9	67
10	Chapter 10	74
11	Chapter 11	86
12	Chapter 12	92
13	Chapter 13	103
14	Chapter 14	110
15	Chapter 15	118
16	Chapter 16	123
17	Chapter 17	131
18	Chapter 18	140
19	Chapter 19	150
20	Chapter 20	157
21	Phorbas' Files	First	173
22	Phorbas' Files	Finish	178
Epilogue		184
About the Author		188

1

Chapter 1

Even a tiny seed can grow into something mighty. It just has to refuse to stay buried.

A memory of Dad's voice reverberates in my head, bouncing off every wall of my skull that I am increasingly convinced is empty of any actual gray matter. There is piercing tinnitus in my left ear and my cheek stings to the touch. Aside from the pain, all I feel is annoyance. Am I really this naive?

I reach up to see if my head is bleeding or just nervously sweating. An ample greasy mixture of both, I'd say. Planting myself back into reality, I look across this claustrophobic cave to search for my belongings. My flashlight has somehow ended up on the opposite side of the cave mouth from me with its lamp still burning, illuminating the dusty haze stretching miles into the earth. There is only one way into this rocky crevice and only one way out. It sure would be a lot easier if *in* is the path our beast has chosen while I was so unceremoniously incapacitated, but the way this hunt has gone, I doubt it.

While gathering my thoughts and wondering where in the world my hat might have landed, a shadow begins to creep up the rockbound walls. A little too tired to feel fear fully, my curiosity elongates my spine from my seated position among the pebbles. This creature, stepping slowly out of the darkness of the night sky and into the light of my disarmed torch, is accompanied by an anxious ticking sound. This nagging noise is still a bit muffled sounding to me, but it grows louder and louder as the beast approaches. It begins to clank with every step, almost as if it is armor-clad. I scramble to my hands and knees to try and find somewhere, anywhere, to hide from what could be the dweller of this den.

The only sanctuary I manage to find is between a large stone and the concave wall. Keeping my movements small and my breath controlled, I never lose sight of this approaching monster. This monster is now casting a vast shadow on the silt floor. The beast is standing inches in front of my light and not moving a muscle, almost as if it knows I am here. Can it smell me?

I am woefully unprepared for an astute nose at the moment. This aroma of iron emanating from the stains on my duck cloth jacket might be confused with a porterhouse steak to something hungry enough. Maybe the rotting vermin bones strewn about the place will help mask the stench of the rotten lump of anxiety in my throat. From the blinding backlight, I can only see the creature's silhouette. The mystery monster is on all fours. They're stocky with a canine-shaped muzzle and a small tail that is swaying back and forth like it's searching for something. It's low to the ground with blocky shoulders.

Wait a second.

"Geiger, if that's you, so help me," my whisper echoes louder than I'd like.

Just then, the creature rears up to stand on its hind legs, and

CHAPTER 1

the ticking sound ceases. Beams of green light shoot out of its eyes and begin scanning the corridor to find me. I raise my hand to block the double beams that are now blinding me. Can't hear right, can't see shit, can't wait for this night to be over.

A robotic voice hums out from the beast, "Eric! There you are. It smells terrible in here. I love pretending to smell."

Yep, that's Geiger.

"Why are you hiding?" she asks. "Are we now the ones being hunted?" She swivels at the hips and holds her front paws up like she's an action movie hero. "Should I initiate protocol," a noise like a jukebox finding its cassette sounds, and then a tape recording of a man's voice rings out, "'*RUN LIKE HELL, BOYS'?*" Her usual speaking voice returns to apologize for her aggressive language, "Sorry for cursing."

I sigh with relief. "No, G. They got me with a classic hit-and-run." I stand to my feet with a slight imbalance that I try not to let her see. "Did ya have to make such an ominous entrance? You nearly gave me a heart attack."

"Cardiac concerns," her eyes and ears perk up a bit too eagerly for my liking. "Do you require defibrillator assistance?" Her core warbles, and her plastic joints begin to glow like lightning strikes around the edges.

"No! I mean, no, thank you." I dial my tone back before it deserves a good jolt. "I didn't know you had that party trick."

"As Dr. Carpenter would say, '*LITTLE BODY, BUT BIG BATTERY.*'" My mother's telephonic voice echoes out of Geiger and down the stone cavern.

"I'm sorry for runnin' ahead — got a little carried away," I grimace while smoothing out my face, hoping to regain some feeling.

"That's a-okay," she assures. "We should never contain our

excitement. Now, let me examine your bloody cranium. The bleeding surely has clotted by now."

She clunkily pokes around my head like a maternal silverback gorilla checking her young for ticks. Her paw brushes over an old scar that is buried under my mop of black hair. Even after all these years, I still recoil if something unexpected touches that spot. In her defense, it is a large scar that runs from the crown of my head to my widow's peak. It would be hard to check my scalp and not find it.

If I weren't already concussed, I would say she's doing more harm than good by waving those android mitts around, but she was right. The gash on the side of my head had stopped bleeding and was beginning to scab.

"It's looking a-okay," Geiger says, all chipper. "You've always been a fast healer."

"Yeah, well, that doesn't mean I like your clunky fingers near my open woun— ouch!"

"Whoops," she says. "Must have been my clunky fingers."

I roll my eyes at the dirt so she doesn't see.

"Dr. Carpenter requires that I assess all of your wounds," she continues. "She is concerned for you and how this rapid healing may have come to be."

"She's my mom," I reply. "Of course, she wants you to look at all my bumps and scrapes. If she was that worried about it, she'd do it herself."

"Your mother works very hard. She built me to tend to you in moments when she is unavailable. Assisting you with cryptid hunting was a nice bonus innovation."

I swat my hand at those nagging words I've heard a million times. "I know, I know. But I'm not some test subject, ya know. I'm her son. She wants you to report back on my wounds so that she can formulate a scientific method or something. I don't know."

"Wrong," Geiger flatly replies. "She wants me to report on your wounds because when you get them, you do not report them."

"Remember that time my clavicle fracture healed in, like, what, forty minutes?" I ask. "By the time I fill out the incident report, it's as if there was no incident to begin with."

"The foundation needs you to be in top shape. This includes knowing when you are injured in the field."

She's a company gal, I'll give her that. But she's not hearing me.

"They're worried about damaged goods," I clarify. "Making me wear this shit uniform, making you wear a collar; it's all about possession with them. They care about *our* wellbeing because it affects *their* wellbeing. I fear that's how Mom views us, too— ouch!"

"Whoops," Geiger says with a grin. "Must have been my '*CLUNKY FINGERS.*'"

I would tell Geiger to remind me not to walk right up to a sasquatch next time I have one cornered, but she would likely remind me by using another recording of my own voice against me, which is, admittedly, hilarious and humiliating.

"Are ya getting any rad readings?" I ask, hoping to put an end to this lecture disguised as a triage.

"Of course!" she says. "Do you require readings on the beast that did this to you or readings on the beast that I followed, which led to you?"

My mouth drops open as angels and demons fight among themselves on my shoulders over who will speak for me next. I can tell my mother designed Geiger because she always seems to deliver the bad news last, or not at all, if unprompted. What would mankind be without its best friend? I think my blood pressure would be more consistent, but I guess I would miss her. The angel wins for now.

"You're saying there are *two* beasts nearby?"

"At least," she confirms in her always optimistic tone.

Grabbing my flashlight, I begin stuffing my backpack with all the things that were flung out of it: two electric bolas, my 8-track player along with a couple of cartridges, my net launcher, and two spare batteries. Mom's team invented my tools, except the music stuff, of course. She never liked the idea of me being a seeker, but it upped her tech game, wanting to make sure I stayed alive while chasing cryptids all hours of the night.

When I was in kindergarten, I wanted to be a firefighter, but that did not last long. It would only be a few short years later that cryptids would earn their permanent place in my life. Besides, if this bustling, obnoxiously perfect city ever discovered the existence of even one snallygaster, their tidy white picket-fenced homes and apple pies cooling in the windows would never again be in order. Knowing that the '*smartest*' creature is no longer at the top of the food chain would be enough for hair pomade and canned wine to be out of stock at the markets for months. And not only for their peace of mind but also for their safety.

Cryptids can be violent, especially in territory that makes them feel displaced, a truth I know too well. If some Tom, Dick, or Harry thinks he's got what it takes to hang a jackalope from his mantle, people will start risking their lives beyond the Spikes just for trophies. The Hyde Foundation and seekers like me are unknown to the masses, but we keep them safe from themselves and things completely unseen.

CHAPTER 1

Like the beasts, I despise coming out of the countryside and into this town. It's unusual for me to be in this sector but even more unusual for an eight-hundred-pound land mammal to be here. Bigfoots are as described: big. How one has managed to be so close to the metro area and not found its way onto the local news in a grainy instant camera photograph is beyond me. Then again, how they ever get through the Spikes is a mystery we have yet to solve. And as my dog double has so timely informed me, there could be more than one beast in the area. The only thing more unlikely than that is her being wrong.

I throw one strap of my pack over my shoulder with a groan and knock the soot off of my hat to place it back on my head. "We're chasing the moon at this point already," I say. "Which way are ya pointing us?"

Geiger's rad counter hums back to life in a tizzy. "The largest concentration of radiation leads out of this cave," she says, "and toward the tree line, east. Starting the hunt anew, what a wonderful opportunity."

A little bit back toward the outskirt neighborhoods, but the half-moon should keep us shrouded well enough. We step out of the cave mouth, and I breathe a diaphragm's worth of fresh air, my first in what feels like hours. Maybe this time I can talk some sense into this 'squatch.

Chapter 2

We begin hiking back down the path that had previously led us up to the cave. Occasionally, we slow down to ensure the sets of tracks are headed the same way we are and to ensure the tracks are not so obviously left by an 8-foot-tall primate. Hiding beasts is one thing; cleaning up after them is another. I'm glad that the clean-up portion isn't my job.

We quickly find ourselves off the gravelly paths and into the forest. There is no darkness quite like midnight under a thick wooded canopy. Every chirp and croak gets a quick brush of my flashlight just to be sure it's not a creature of concern. It's amazing how perfectly natural sounds and sights are made eerily unsettling just by encasing them in the mystery of limited vision. G has her headlamps on ahead of me.

Following Geiger through the woods like this reminds me of when we were kids. I mean, Geiger's an ageless canine android, but I was a kid. The forest at night was never scary to me. I loved the chorus of crickets and frogs that made the dead of night prove it's life. I loved how the stars overhead revealed themselves in abounding number the further we got from the glow of our front porch light. I loved chasing after the lightning bugs and watching them as they turned the forest into its own sea of stars. Reaching out and catching them made me feel special, as if I could hold the very stars in my hands.

Most of all, I loved camping by the creek bed with Dad and making a campfire under the full moon in a small clearing. The trees were like mighty sentinels that shielded us from the rest of the world. My dad was just like those giant redwoods that insulated us — unwavering in the wind and roots planted so deep you could never dig them up. He was barrel-chested with calloused working hands like bear paws. He taught me how to catch lightning bugs, how to be fast enough to snag them but gentle enough not to harm them. Even though most of my memories of him are like trying to watch a slideshow that barely survived a house fire, I miss him every day.

Bumping my knee into Geiger's chunky plastic exterior brings me sprinting back from my leisurely walk down memory lane. She is standing like a parody of a short-haired pointer with her nose to the ground and her ears up on alert. Her eyes are fixed on a deserted shed. A rust-devoured garage door is left half open. There is no light coming from inside, only a safety light outside hung on the nearest electric pole.

Geiger darts her eyes at me in a look that says, "This is it." She is normally cheery and chatty, but when it comes to seeking, she tries her best to put on a serious face. When she begins to act like a real dog — no speaking and using her ears to guide her — I know the time for games is over.

I sit my pack down behind a tree and grab one of my bolas out of it. They are shaped like softballs without the stitched seams. When flung, this softball shape splits in two, connected only by an arc of hot blue electricity. The voltage is enough to zap some aggression out of whatever they contact, making them a little more agreeable by the time they hit the ground. The same can be said for the net that fires out of the launcher, but that's better for smaller targets than what we are after tonight. I love hunting large targets. The adrenaline of monstrous pursuits really gets the blood running. Small cryptids can pose a threat, especially in large groups, but there's no better hunt than bagging a true monstrosity.

When tracking *Magnus pes* — or bigfoot — it's important to keep yourself slow and low. Their eyes survey the land, looking for horizontal movement, so unless you can move from treetop to treetop, you'd better keep your speed and silhouette in mind. The sasquatch does not have any natural predators, and this way of seeing the land mostly helps them hunt agile varmints. If we don't want to become the hunted ourselves, we will need to be careful. Geiger will stay outside and alert me if the beast bolts. As for me, I'm going inside the destitute dormitory to flush him out. Stalking around gets old quickly. I'm ready for some action.

With bent knees, I slowly walk my way to the back entrance of the garage. The woods have grown dangerously devoid of sound. There's no noise that I can hear from the bigfoot, and not even the crickets are chirping. Seekers have been taught that when the forest falls silent, you should be at your most alert; even a miserable mosquito knows when it oughtta keep its buzzing to a minimum.

Using my flashlight would give me away immediately, so I'm going to have to do my best without it. As I slither into the garage door, I pull the solid steel as close to closed as I can. In the vaguely existent moonlight coming through the high

CHAPTER 2

windows, I can make out an old automobile and an ice box on the opposite side of the room from me.

The deafening quiet has me waiting to move even an inch. The only sound I hear is my racing heartbeat. It would be dangerous to enter any further without first having a sense of where this behemoth is. There seems to be a grease pit beneath where this old vehicle is sitting. If there is a sasquatch down there, he likely has already seen me.

I wasn't lying when I said the dark didn't scare me, but knowing that a giant monster is potentially in that darkness waiting for me to let my guard down, well, that's a different fear. Assuming that he is hiding from me there, I creep my way around to the front of the vehicle. If he is going to ambush me, I'd like to at least be able to have an engine block between me and him. I'll take any advantage I can get.

The palms of my hands are swamps. My pupils are vest buttons. Your body can sense survival moments, and my senses are peaking. The unknowing of how such a large creature can be watching me in this small space without being the least bit detectable weighs on me as though the monster sits on my very shoulders. My breaths shorten. In my left hand is my flashlight that will certainly reveal me to him, but it might also give me a small reprieve from feeling like the prey. It's stupid, but that small relief is worth more to me than my own life at this moment.

Suspecting still that the creature is in the grease pit, I raise my quaking arm and point my torch into the black abyss. With one flip of a switch, I will have my answer. After closing my eyes and taking a slow, full breath, I flick the lamp on. My eyes adjust to the newfound light in the engulfing darkness, but there is nothing to be seen. My heart rises out of my stomach back to its normal resting place. A brush of air in a chuckle of relief escapes my nose. If he is in here, he sees me now. Yet still, the garage is silent.

Cautiously, I stand to my feet and slowly sweep the bulbs glow across the room like a lighthouse warning sailors of the approaching shore. First, in the direction I entered from and then around to the far side. Now feeling confident in my solitude, I turn around to check the corners that were previously neglected by the moonlight. Nothing. Still nothing.

Geiger is usually never wrong about these things. I raise my light to see the ceiling, wondering if turning the overhead lights on would even have an effect in this rusty shack. It's then that I notice that I am not looking at the ceiling but rather the flat underbelly of a wooden loft. The angle of the moon shining through the glass never revealed this higher level to me. Before I have time to react, I see two dark eyes reflecting my lamp light back at me.

The hands of this creature are gripped to the edge of the loft. The skin on his hands is coarser than leather. He is perched on the edge as if he had been planning to drop down on me from above. The hair on his head is stood up. His eyes are blacker than the void of night being kept at bay. Not knowing if I should be fighting or flighting, I freeze. His face is snarled to the point that his inch-long canines are exposed, but perhaps the stun of light now blasting in his corneas has given me a sliver of a second to act. Without thinking, I bolt toward the door.

A loud crash booms behind me, accompanied by a visceral gargling roar. I hit the back door with my shoulder to barge it open. As it swings shut behind me, I glance back to see the sasquatch barge into that same steel door with so much force that it is removed from its hinges. His stride is unaffected as he swings his heavy hands ahead of him to paw the dirt beneath him and extract as much forward aggression as the loose earth allows. If it's a foot race, I have already lost.

Geiger comes peeling around the far side of the building. She stands under the safety light, knowing that she awaits my signal. As I weave in and out of trees to gain any ground possible on my pursuer, sounds of splintering bark remind me that this beast does not need to take my course with the same caution. Slightly losing my footing on the leafy forest floor, a plan conjures in my mind.

Quick, small movements are my only chance. Big and strong as they may be, a bigfoot's lack of agility could be my one physical advantage. I cut hard right, my momentum switching directions in a blink. The sasquatch bellows as his fully extended sledge of an arm brushes so close to my skin that I feel the force of the wind almost knock me off balance. The cryptid slams its side on a tree trunk while trying to match my maneuver. This small collision gives me enough room to stride toward Geiger. Poor sucker doesn't know what's about to hit him.

The beast's pursuit is not over. He is back after me but headed exactly where we want him. Geiger, standing on her hind legs, has my other bola ready to be deployed. I stand in front of her to keep the cryptid's unbroken aggression. He is charging straight for us. My breathing is now more like heaving as the adrenaline of survival begins to wear off.

"On three, G," I manage to blurt out between gasps of air.

She does not reply, and I do not turn around to check on her. What is understood between us does not need to be communicated. We are a team, we are best friends, and I know she has my back.

"One," I stammer.

Slobber from the beast's jowls coats its anguished screeching teeth.

"Two."

Blood from the creature's digging knuckles flings on the pendulum of the creature's gait.

"Three!"

Diving out of the way, the creature nearly halts as it turns, again trying to match me. In that microsecond of its confusion, Geiger launches a bola at the creature's torso. Halfway through the flight, the spherical shape breaks into two. At first, the pieces fly silently through the cool night air, but right before the moment of contact, a thunderous crackle rings out. A blue light flashes brighter than a welder's torch melting titanium.

Deafening and blinding leads to quiet and stillness. The beast lays on the ground, breathing in airy gulps, but finally down.

I crawl backward until my hand finds something I can lean my weight onto. Finding rest at the base of the light pole, my body is quivering as the chemicals in my brain work to balance out my previous neglect of self-preservation.

That was close. If that monster had dropped his frame on me from above, there's nothing I could've done about it. If he had been a step faster, I might have had a second wound that would require scar tissue. The unsettling reality of my situation sinks in as my nervous thoughts have me in a downward spiral. I've worked for years on my body and mind to be tougher than brass, but life is life, and death is death. Small errors get you killed in this animal kingdom I belong to, some days you have to get lucky. But the job is done, so I can push all that down for now till the next close call.

"Great job!" Geiger says. "You had some really amazing

CHAPTER 2

moves."

"Damn straight, couldn't have done it without ya," I throw out in exhaustion. "Just need to catch my breath."

"Do not forget we have the net launcher if you need assistance with *catching* your breath." She looks at me sideways with the slyest eyes. She knows how horrible that joke was, but she also knows that a bad joke is the grounding in reality that I need right now. "A little slower, and you would have been *sasquashed*."

"Okay, that's enough," I say, with the slightest corner of a smile raised. "We should Morse this one in, let the clean-up crew know it's safe to come out of *Hyding*," I *pun*-ch back at her.

She nods and pats my shoulder. "Yes, we should. But your beast communication could use the extra practice while we have a test subject."

I was hoping she would say that. Earlier this same night, I attempted to speak with this 'squatch. Like a drunken night for a would-be Casanova, it ended with zero replies and a smack on the side of my head. Mom knows about my accelerated healing, but my ability to communicate with the cryptids is a secret from everyone. If I can't throw you, I don't trust you, and Geiger launches easier than most.

I love my mom, but her love for research might take precedence over me. It feels wrong to even think that she would treat me like a lab rat, but then why do I feel hesitant to tell her? Instinct has kept me alive before, and perhaps it is keeping me out of an ass-less patient's gown now.

A grumble and a slight crunch of leaves remind me that the beast is only stunned. I get back on my feet and carefully approach him. He is mostly lifeless, exhausted, undoubtedly.

There's a smell of fried hair coming off him with an almost

visible aura due to the smoke emanating from where the bola made contact. Clouded in that smell is a tinge of blood and saliva. The more I examine the true effect of the bola, the more I realize why he attacked me. Did he somehow recognize I was with the Hyde Foundation? Did he know that I potentially could have the power of a storm cloud in my pocket? I wouldn't speak to me either if that were the case. Still, it is unusual for me not to hear a word from him through all of this. I kneel beside him, this time remembering to stay out of arm's reach.

"Hey, remember me?" I ask the beast.

His eyes open, but there is no reply. There is no color in his iris, only inky black.

"My skull nearly had your handprint embossed on it? Ringing any bells? Besides mine."

Something like realization crosses his expression. Similar to showing a bundle of bananas to a zoo monkey. His eyes are glossed over. He is trying to examine me, but clearly, he is looking through a fog, still reeling from our shock therapy methods.

My ability to speak to beasts is not universal. What makes a beast a *cryptid* is not its mysterious origins; if it were, I'd have a lot of questions for platypuses. Cryptids come from the other side of the Spikes, a mountain range so high and vast that this entire city, the countryside, all of it, is built in its basin. The jagged mountain walls tower to the clouds, literally protecting all of us within from powerful radiation storms. Hence, Geiger counters are used to track things that are not from our side of the wall.

Nothing in this basin could survive a day in those Radlands, but these creatures can. Their cells crave radiation. It affects them differently than humans and leads to unnatural expansive growth. My speaking ability does not apply to your average animal, only cryptids. My current theory is the radiation itself. Something about it and how it affects the creatures. Maybe it advances their minds beyond that of an animal but not quite to the level of a human. It's all guesswork for now.

I wave my hand in front of the bigfoot's face to see if his eyes track me at all. Slowly, they start to follow my direction. I make another attempt to speak with him, "Anybody home, big guy?"

His ocular abysses stare blankly at me. After a pause, he raises his stare to my head, to my hat. I see the reflection in his eye of the big metallic *H* logo. It lights a new fire within him. A growl gurgles out. I take a few steps back. His hands have found their way beneath his frame as he uses all of his strength to hoist his body up from the dirt. The creature snarls in pain as he gets his feet beneath him. Hitting him with another bola would feel cruel, but it's swiftly becoming my only option.

"Don't do this, man," I plead with the creature. "Can't we talk about it?"

My grip tightens on the bola that I pull from my pocket. Zapping him again in such rapid succession to the first might do permanent damage. These tools were made to subdue efficiently, not be tossed around like children's toys. I'm not one to pull punches on feral beasts, but that doesn't mean I want to maim them, either. He is slowly rising back up to his feet. He is on one knee, trying to reclaim his fighting spirit from the grips of fifty-thousand volts.

Cocking my arm back, I let out a final appeal. "I don't wanna hurt you, dumbass, but I ain't about to have you chasing me around anymore, either!"

An ear-shattering roar tells me all I need to know: he is not in a talking mood. My internal war rages on, but if it is between another chase sequence or shocking him one more time, I will make the decision that leads to less cardio. Out of the corner of my eye, as if it were in slow motion, I notice a flake falling.

Snow? That can't be. It's chilly, don't get me wrong, but snow doesn't stand a chance. The beast seems to notice it, too, as he looks up toward the clouds overhead. It is not just a flake anymore. This substance is filling the air around us both. His cheeks soften, and his shoulders droop. He thuds back onto the ground with a roar. No, a snore. Is he asleep?

My face toward the sky, my words toward Geiger, I say, "Please tell me this is some new tech I forgot to ask you about."

"Apologies," she replies, "the source of this powder is unidentifi—"

A whoosh of wind silences her mid-sentence and blows my hat clean off my head. I turn to face the direction of the gust. My eyes are adjusted to the enlightened area beneath the safety light. Everything outside of this small glow is pure black. My mind thinks of the bigfoot as my eyes scan for any horizontal movement. My eyes yank my view upward to study the source of another strong burst of wind. This one knocks me to the ground. Geiger and I, on the same eye level now, are facing toward the tree line. From behind us, though, I hear a calm, scratchy query.

"Human, how is it that I may understand your tongue?"

Chapter 3

My neck hair is standing on end, and turning around is the last thing I want to do. My natural instinct is working overtime for me today. Cutting my wide eyes over at Geiger, I see she has her hands up like the police are detaining us.

Her internal jukebox is whirring again, searching for another 8-track recording. *"WE WILL GIVE YOU ANYTHING YOU WANT, JUST DON'T SHOOT!"*

I am never letting her watch Westerns again. She cannot understand what the beast said, but she undoubtedly heard his eerie chortle. Does a tingle run up an android's spine?

The mystery voice calls out to us again. "You can understand me, can you not, brother?"

I stand cautiously, playing cool by knocking dirt and debris off the front side of my pants. My expression braces for some unknown impact, and my shoulders slightly shrug to raise my arms to match Geiger's immediate physical admission of defeat. My squinted eyes widen to take in the grim truth that is standing in front of me. Standing before me is a myth. Standing before me is an impossibility. Standing before me is T*inea magna* — the great moth — the mothman.

He stands like he's been preparing for this reveal all night, directly in the spotlight of the electric pole and hands tucked into the pockets of his trench coat. His eyes are giant and the richest version of scarlet and so reflective that the smallest light appears to make them glow. His necktie matches his eyes, and the rest of his tailored garments match his midnight and ash-colored body, save for a dingy white button-up. A pattern, like swirling peacock feathers, coats the wings that wrap down to his sides. His feet are like owl claws. Otherwise, I think they'd be in a pair of Oxfords.

I have heard the myths of such a monster, but not a single story prepared me for the wannabe noir detective I see now. Recalling the stories makes my fists clench and my face depart from color. Never has there been a moth sighting that didn't end in tragedy.

Apparently, I should work on my poker face because Geiger takes one look at me and has to see for herself. If she makes even one joke about him being able to eat his own suit if he ever gets hungry, we might become moth food ourselves. To my surprise, she does not speak. Her face tightens with her brow. She is just as unsure as I am.

Desperately needing to break the tension in the air, I reply to him while faking a stiff spine. "Sure seems that way. Out for a midnight flight?"

The face of the moth remains expressionless if it is even capable of expression. Besides his eyes and a mouth that opens every once in a while, it's hard to make out his features. The fur on his face is so dark that it hides the intricate shapes of his identity.

CHAPTER 3

"My, my," the moth says, "that is quite curious. Where do tell, have you acquired such a skill?"

His teeth are like needle points packed together tighter than rows of corn.

"There's nothin' to tell," I reply. "It's just somethin' I can do."

My answer may not suffice, and I delivered it in a nervous tone that could be confused with a lie, but it is the truth.

"Born understanding the speech of monsters? In 200 years of life, you are the first of a kind. Has nature made you special, or perhaps nurture?"

Trying to tell what occupies his ogle is a waste of time. His eyes have not blinked, and they are staring holes directly ahead as if he is lost in thought on the edge of the world. His head tilts slightly to let me know he is, in fact, evaluating something.

"Purple pigment dicing through your obsidian hair," he observes of me. "Born with that abnormality as well? Two in one does not a coincidence make."

It is not my best hair day, but why does he care what color it is? My hair is indeed split down the middle by a purple color. At the root of this patch is my scar, I have always attributed the rough skin combined with the rapid healing for the weird unnatural hue. This is beginning to feel like an interrogation.

"No, not necessarily," I say. "I have a scar on my head. It messes with how some of my hair looks."

"You know what they say about scars and stories; some are deeper than others. At what depth do you bury the story of this violet scar?"

If I didn't know any better, I'd say this moth is just as pleased to have found a human he can speak to as I am to have confirmed a new species. He's full of questions, but I'm not sure I have the answers he's looking for.

"There was an accident when I was younger," I say. "I can't remember much of it; that happens in head trauma. The amnesia's a blessing if ya ask me."

The moth's eyes are mesmerizing. I'm not sure if he has a hypnotic effect on me or if my disbelief keeps me from looking away. Oh, hypnotic effect, that reminds me.

"How did you do that?" I ask, pointing at the downed beast.

"A simple sleep spore." The moth shakes his wings to show how the dust falls off them. "A gift of moths, the spores. See, we are both special in our own ways."

"I was standing in that mist, too, right? How'd you make it only affect him and not me?"

The moth smiles. The gnarliest curl of a smile, but a smile nonetheless. "Finally, brother, you ask something worthy of an answer."

The moth is proper and polite, but he either just called me dumb, ignorant, or naive, and I'm not sure which one I'd prefer. Speaking to creatures is a gift of mine, but never have I spoken to one so articulate, and so well dressed, or so well behaved for that matter. If he was still hiding in the shroud of night, I would not know he was a beast at all. Great moths are myths to me; well, they were five minutes ago. I can't let this moment of discovery cause me to lose sight of the situation. My priority needs to be determining if I'm in any danger.

"I am not your enemy, seeker," the moth says. "You can quiet your mind."

You can read my mind, I say internally, my mouth slightly agape as I wait for his reply. The crickets seem to have started back up with their violin playing.

"Do stop staring at me like that, won't you?" he asks. "It's not often a moth gets a chill on the spine. You are wondering my intentions, no?"

So he can't read my mind. I stared at him a little too long there, awkward. If he *could* read my thoughts, it wouldn't take him long.

"You are near the city, and you really shouldn't be," I say. "But somethin' tells me you're not exactly lost either."

A grin looks very menacing on him, but I think he means no harm. "Correct," he answers. "Actually, I was looking for you. The *Hyde* seeker that speaks to the hidden."

He points to my hat with the Hyde Foundation logo on its crown. The Seekers have just become the sought. Does he hate us and want me dead? Is he looking for something?

"You need a seeker?" I ask. "What for?"

The moth chitters; I think that's how he laughs. "Come now, seeker. Does it appear that I need help with *finding*? Found you, did I not? You could barely locate the bigfoot hiding out in the attic."

He makes a good point, but that still was uncalled for.

"We do not have much time," he says. "Your companion has likely signaled for your transport home amid this encounter."

Geiger looks a little more relaxed, but her brow remains furrowed. She is waiting for a determination from me, but I haven't quite arrived at one yet.

The mothman continues, "Cryptids sometimes wander too far and go missing from our Radlands; this is true. Recently, however, disappearances have increased hand over fist, and reappearances have dropped nearly to absolute zero. The few that do return often do not return as the same creature that was lost. They are haunted, tormented."

His thousand-yard stare leaves. Now, he is focusing on me,

and there are no misgivings about it. His bug eyes can see the entire world around him. It's uncomfortable being the sole object of their scrutiny. He asks a question directly aimed at me. "You *hiders* and you *seekers* wouldn't happen to know anything about that, would you?"

Beasts are disappearing at a higher rate? But our seeking numbers have remained on pace with our usual quota. Does he think they are getting into Corinth or the Green and just not being discovered? Or is he accusing us of having something to do with the disappearances?

"You think we have somethin' to do with it?" I ask. "We protect your sorry asses from this world and protect this world from your sorry asses in the process. If any beasts were gettin' out of the Spikes, we'd have it under control."

He takes a step toward me, and I immediately retreat myself one step to match.

"Your intentions may be true," he says, "but the intent is often the best-kept lie. Words will never reveal intentions; only actions will do that." His bulging eyes study me for a silent moment more. Is he wondering how many meals he can get out of my skinny body, or is he trying to search me for lies? He breaks his gaze on me and turns it to Geiger. "Tell this dog to take down these coordinates. The two of you will meet me there in two days' time at dusk."

I relay the message to her, hoping that she will know what to say because I sure don't.

"Kindly, sir, we must refuse," Geiger combats. "It was much too scary to meet you once. The anxiety of a second meeting is enough to fry any logical mind. Also, all legends of you '*LEPIDOPTERA*' point to your kind as bad omens. No offense."

When I translate her to the mothman, he lets out a guttural

chitter; this time, it's definitely a laugh. "Are moths harbingers of doom," he begins, "or were they too late to stop the impending doom? Trust me, dog, and hear me, brother; doom is impending. Without you, our meeting might just become another bad omen."

Geiger and I look at each other. Something about how the moth speaks makes me want to trust him. His wisdom and his riddles fascinate me. If he wanted us dead, we would be, yet here we are. He is calling us for an abnormal mission. Do you know how hard it is for a cryptid hunter to be given an abnormal mission? The abnormal transformed itself into normal over time. This day and this night have been exceptional, even by our standards. A small piece of me wants to learn more about him, and a small piece of me wants to help him, but what does Geiger think? Can she keep any of this a secret?

In one last effort, the moth provokes my thoughts and says, "If I were someone who wanted to steer you clear of moths, I would ensure their negative reputation as *bad omens* as well."

Is he implying the legends are fake? Half-truths? The more we talk, the more I get the feeling that he knows the answers to most of this interrogation, and this whole thing was just a formality, a vetting process. He needs me so that he can speak to someone within the Hyde ranks, and he's stringing us along, dangling a carrot of truth in front of our curious noses. This is the most thinking I've done in a long time, but even I know thinking long leads to thinking wrong.

"Give me the coordinates, quick," Geiger demands of me. Her mind is made up for both of us. "Our clean-up crew is close. You must leave now. We will join you at—" she pauses. "We will join you in two nights' time."

Without as much as a nod, the moth leaps into the sky on

sudden flaps of his wings. Outer space must be his exact color, the way he vanishes in the sky of stars.

My face is as pale as the moon, and my head is as light as its gravity. Keeping secrets is becoming part of my DNA. Personal secrets are one thing, but this contact we've had tonight is historic. All the rumors, all the myths, nothing ever first hand has been confirmed. Conviction burns hot in my heart, but which truth is this conviction yearning to keep? Two days is how long I have to think. Two days before we meet him again, this nameless noir. Two days for me to be left alone with my thoughts. Now that's dangerous.

"Where's he want us to go?" I ask Geiger, still searching the clouds for his shape.

"We must prepare properly," she says. "Our services have been requested beyond the Spikes."

Chapter 4

Clean-up has got to be the worst job at the Hyde Foundation. Sweeping away footprints in the dirt, lying to any peering eyes about environmental conservation efforts, and gaslighting witnesses into believing what they saw has a perfectly logical explanation.

No, good citizen, that rabbit did not have horns. It simply had a cancerous growth extending from its sweet little noggin. Sane, rational, handsome citizen, surely you do not believe that an overgrown frog was seen walking on its hind legs. Surely, we tell you, it was an escaped pet iguana raring up in an unfortunate bout of confusion. Clean-up crews are efficient, punctual, and thoroughbred liars. Speaking of punctuality, here comes their truck now.

The sun is threatening to rise at this cool early dawn, and they do not have much time. Five or six cleaners pour out of the truck, all in single file. I'm pretty familiar with most of the cleaners. It aids the overall effort if we keep the teams small. But still feeling slightly in shock and very tired, I didn't look at any of them as they flooded out around me. The first member out takes my incident report immediately so they know how to direct the rest of the crew. Geiger is supposed to be asked to confirm my statement, but for the sake of time, she is often skipped — the girl can be a real rambler, and time is more valuable when you have the least of it to give.

I give them the full rundown of my sasquatch encounter and only the sasquatch encounter. Operation *Dirty Butterfly* is officially a go — yes, Geiger came up with that. While the cleaners begin their various duties, I load up in the truck to await their finish. A job well done rewards me whatever night we have left to simply rest my head on the cold stainless walls of the enclosed truck bed. My job ends, and theirs begins.

Overall, it was a clean night. No witnesses other than the winged one. A straight path of size 28 feet prints leading from the cozy cave I 'napped' in down to the shed our squatch napped near. One bola discharged, no net needed. Is there anything I'm forgetting? It feels like I'm forgetting something. Whatever the case, it can't be that crucial if I can't even think—

My eyes burst open as my heart drops into my intestines. That was a nice five minutes of relaxation while it lasted. I just remembered the sleep spore.

Popping up from my seat, I hang my head out the back hatch doors and survey to see where all the crew has dispersed. Geiger is perched beneath me, doing the same with her next extended comically long hanging out the back of the doorway.

"The coast is clear," she says. "It's now or never."

"Simmer down there, detective," I try to rein in her sense of espionage. "Let's just head toward the light pole. Nothing is up. We are just two seekers walking around our hunting ground. Got it?"

"Two seekers, one secret. I hear you," she slaps my shoulder.

CHAPTER 4

"Stay close to me!"

She flies out of the truck over toward the post where we last left the bigfoot. I start out behind her, trying to keep my pace a nonchalant, fast walk. My focus is on catching up to Geiger. I call out for her to slow down a few times, but naturally, she does not listen. Two cleaners walk past us. They are pushing a gurney with the beast on it. He is still sound asleep. That's a good sign, right? The clean-up crew is taking him to the vehicle to load up; they must not have noticed anything out of the ordinary.

My eyes stop focusing on the two beast pushers and look around again for Geiger. She is standing under the light and next to a cleaner who is kneeling down, running their fingers through the dirt. Uh oh. I stride over on my tip toes in hurried steps.

The cleaner raises a hand to pat Geiger's head, then over their shoulder, they call out to me like honey is on their lips: slow, sweet, and with a little bit of twang. "You weren't gonna tell me?"

I freeze. What did G say in the five seconds it took me to get here? If she bragged about meeting a moth, I will find a luxurious scrap yard to throw her in.

"Eric, come in, Eric. You weren't gonna tell me this mission was you and this good girl?" The cleaner rubs behind Geiger's ears.

Well, I'll be. I know that voice. She turns her head to me, revealing a smile more inspiring than the amber rays of sunlight unveiling a new morning. A silky bun of copper hair sticks out from her snapback cap. Even in that tacky uniform with her olive-colored work shirt tucked into her canvas pants, I find myself captivated.

"Good golly, Miss Molly," I say. "Didn't even see you get off the truck. I must be more out of it than I thought."

She lets out an exaggerated laugh as she rises to her feet. "Ha, I'd say. You two brought down a near half-tonner. One bola, too. Lots of tracks around that shed. He was really diggin'. He likes his big feet so much he didn't wanna come off of 'em, huh?"

"It was a long night, for sure. I'm glad it's over, and we can get outta here. Ready to load up?" I say, putting the art of suggestion at work — it did not work.

Molly is rubbing her neoprene gloved thumb and index finger together, pretending I didn't say anything at all. "I didn't expect this much pollen to be out here," she says.

"Pollen? Oh, really?" my voice cracks, bringing an unwanted highlight to my guilt. "Well, you know these forests, something's always in bloom."

Geiger chimes in, "Pollen, yes, it is pollen on the ground." Very inconspicuous, G. She doubles down before I can kick her to hush up. "I was wondering why I was a sneezing mess. Achoo!"

If this were a cartoon, a dream bubble would be above my head, and I'd be seen smashing a mallet on Geiger's dome.

Molly sees through the expertly crafted guise and says, "You don't have a respiratory system. If you're sneezing from this pollen, we're all doomed."

Molly's voice is soft as rain and innocent as puppy love, but she's no idiot. Don't confuse her drawl with naivety. She's sharp as a tack and has no quarrel with poking your side with said tack.

"Sun's threatening to shine," Molly breaks the silence. "Better head back." She takes her disposable glove off and shoves it in her pocket.

The three of us make our way to the truck, where the rest of the crew is plenty ready to leave. Our cryptid is fastened in, and trash bags of small animal bones add to the stink of the place. The sights and the smells fade after a while of riding around in it. Plus, once Me and Molly get going, we are in a world where only we exist.

We grew up together in the Hyde labs. Her parents have been with the foundation for about as long as mine have. The mischief we got up to in Mom's research lab or out in the Green with the lab's toys is a miracle that both of us still have our faculties and phalanges. Boys and girls tend to grow apart as they grow up. If they don't end up together, like their parents hope, it's natural to go your own ways. When I started down the seeker path, my self-isolation worsened. Seekers work alone. I have Geiger, but robot dogs don't count as human interaction.

Molly was always so talkative. She was the social butterfly of the two of us. Ironically, if she was a butterfly, it would be fitting to say I was a moth — similar in many ways but crucially different in outward displays. What's important is that I am so proud of her and always love when we can reconnect on hunts. She's one of the few people who would argue that I am not an introvert, and that makes me feel seen for who I am, which is always a warm feeling.

"Do you remember when we tried running away?" I ask Molly.

"Yes, be so for real," she says. "I had my bike loaded up, and here you come on a skateboard. A hundred miles from Corinth, and you bring a skateboard."

"Hey, in my defense, I was confident in those trucks. They were brand new."

"Even if the board held up," she begins, "there's no way you would have. We got, what, a mile from your porch, and you were beggin' to go back."

"Traveling a mile while only kicking to propel yourself forward is admirable, I think."

"Admirable? Wow, never thought of it that way. I was too busy going slow enough to keep up with you that all of my focus was on keeping my balance. I basically walked a mile with a bike between my legs. Now that's admirable."

I laugh because she's right. She's always had to slow down to keep up with me. "Do you ever wish we had done it?" I ask her. "For real."

"What? Run away?" Molly rolls her head from side to side on the truck's metal walls. "No. We got it made here, don't we? Not to mention, it takes us hours to *drive* to Corinth, let alone kickflip to it."

My gaze is low, and I don't want to raise it to hers; I just play with the callouses on my hands. "Do we? Have it made, I mean. Everything we need, but is it everything we want?"

"Don't even start with that bull sugar," she says, refusing to say 'shit.' "Since when does Eric Carpenter know what he wants?"

"This sasquatch will have more freedom than us in a few days," I say. "We catch 'em, then release 'em to a thousand miles of God knows what. All I'm saying is, when do we get released?"

"It's a job," Molly says, "an exclusive job, sure — but still just a job. You are nobody's prisoner. If you want to olley your way off into the sunset, you go right ahead."

Shaking my head, I catch a glimpse out the window. I didn't realize how far we had made it. The ride home always feels faster than the ride out.

Getting through the city's metro area takes hours, even longer if you are unlucky enough to come through right after businesses close. Coming through before most people are even awake is our usual itinerary. Once you fight your way through the city, the roads begin to decrease from six lanes on either side down to two, then down to one, until we are rolling on nothing but single gravel rock lanes.

The Green extends for hundreds of miles in a radius around the city, and the Hyde HQ is south of the city on the greatest length of the Green. We are physically as far away from the bustle as we can be without actually going over the walls ourselves, and that's just the way I like it. There's enough room inside the Spikes to live a full life and never see their jagged, towering sides. I bet half the people in Corinth never have. But some of us who prefer the more rural, quieter life nearly live in their shadow.

When we finally arrive back at the Hyde Foundation, the gate of the barbed fence swings open to greet us. Beyond the fence is a checkpoint, but it never stops us. They only ever stop visitors or anyone sent from the city. The Hyde Foundation is technically a non-profit focusing on wildlife conservation efforts — technically. Dr. Hyde, the founding father, so to speak, made his money selling new-age cassette tech; instant print cameras, 8-track tapes, and VHS films are lumped in there somewhere. He is an intelligent man with great notoriety that he can leverage to get other great minds to join his cause.

Of course, the real work that goes on here is secret. Donors do not know, the city officials do not know, this is an entirely private outfit that only Hyde's most trusted people can be a part of. He and my mother go back about as far as me and Molly. They were lab partners from middle school volcanoes all the way to PhD robotics. There is a lab that guests and visitors are shown full of insects, reptilians, and bird cages. But the real lab, the lab on level minus-one, that's where the real work is.

The compound, as I call it, is huge. That barbed fence surrounds this modern white building about a hundred yards out in each direction. A large dome-shaped observatory in the middle really drives home the *sciencey* look. There are two wings that extend to either side of the dome room: the living quarters and the labs.

Most work can be done on the normal lab floors, we rarely get visitors but even when we do it's not like the common man could visibly tell the difference in turkey feathers and thunderbird feathers anyways. Each wing is three floors high, of course, with a level minus-one secretly beneath the surface. The entrance that we take in the truck loops around to the back of the building, where a loading bay opens to allow us to drive straight into the underground level. It is a long tunnel that winds around and cannot be seen from the front of the building, secrecy and all. Do not be fooled by the *one* part of level minus-one. This level of the foundation is larger than everything above the surface.

Driving into the bay, you are greeted with forklifts and doctors on standby for returning crews. Beyond this entry point is a great open lab floor where researchers can collaborate on findings, as well as several places to house cryptids while we keep them for processing before release. It's a rule of thumb to never hold a cryptid longer than a week, no matter the study or health care provided, which is why it is so unusual for the moth to say reappearances have dwindled. Maybe certain monsters he is looking for are all still in holding with us, but I'm sure there is a good reason, and they will be taken to the Spikes soon enough.

Surrounding the chunky white computers, microscopes, and Petri dishes are smaller lab offices meant for the higher-up

CHAPTER 4

hiders. My mom has her own private lab outfitted with a security code and all. She does not live in the living quarters like me, though. Most grunt-level employees — seekers, cleaners, maintenance, cafeteria — all live on the compound because we are on call twenty-four hours and seven days a week.

The researchers under Dr. Hyde, aptly coined *hiders,* or *Hyders,* if you're nasty, can come and go as they please. Mom found herself a nice neighborhood a bit closer to actual civilization. I don't visit her much there, but she basically visits me every day, with her office being a measly elevator ride away from my 'home.' Is it really living on your own if your mom still checks in on you like your room is still just down the hall from hers?

Now that I'm this close to my bed, I yearn more and more for its sweet embrace. The bags under my eyes could hold groceries enough for a family of four. We drive around to the underneath loading dock, and that 'put your shoes on' feeling makes me reach up tall for a stretch. If there is one thing our foundation is good at, it's delegating. My job is to seek, and once sought, my job is over. When they crack the back hatch open, I step out and let my extended legs shake off any traveling cramps. The reception crew meets us to offload our cargo.

"Good job tonight, sir," Molly says, knocking my shoulder with her fist. "You'd better head up to nap off that *sasquashing* you almost got."

"You don't have to tell me twice," I say. "And don't clean up too good; getting caught is fun every once in a full moon."

She rolls her eyes as she helps unload bags reeking of rot. She stops me from walking away when she calls out, "I'll hunt you down, ya know?"

"I'm the seeker here," I reply. "What are you talking about?"

"If you run away on that skateboard. I still have my bike.

Won't take me long to catch up."

I give her a laugh — not a real one, just one of those where you kind of smile and exhale some air through your nose — as I turn to leave the cleaners to it.

Geiger and I head past a row of holding cells and up the stairs at the far end of the minus-one bay toward the living quarters. My feet feel like they've been dried in cement. I pound my way heavily up the steps. As I reach the top, so close to my unconscious freedom, I nearly bump my lowered head into someone in a white coat.

"Woof, my boy is tired." I hear a familiar voice say.

"Hey, Mom," cackles out of my tired, scratchy throat. "If you ever give up studying and start seeking, be sure to work on your cardio."

"So I've heard," Mom says. "Radio said we bagged a bigfoot. You know what they say about big feet?"

I throw my head back in anguishing embarrassment at the joke I have to hear every time we talk about sasquatches. "Big gait, I know, I know. Mom, I am about to be out on my feet. Please. You and Geiger can chat it up if you'd like."

"LITTLE BODY, BUT BIG BATTERY," Geiger plays out, reminding Mom of her endurance as opposed to mine.

"Good girl, G," Mom says with a head pat for Geiger. "Head on to bed then, and good work tonight. Maybe G can even let me in on how close you and Molly sat on the ride back."

"Peas in a pod," Geiger blurts out like the gossip she is, or rather the both of them are.

Too worn out to care about their pestering, I wave over my shoulder with a dismissive motion and leave them to their tea time.

Finally, peace and quiet. Reaching the topmost section of

minus-one, I punch in my elevator code to call one down for me. The upbeat chimes of the elevator music are a stark contrast to my waning eyelids. The doors slide open with a ding as I reach my floor, the third floor, with the least people and the best view.

Left and right, I walk past sealed rotating doors. I stop at mine and hold my eye up to the retina scan. It doesn't respond until I use my hand to pull my cheek down and reveal more of my eye, but eventually, the sealed door spins open. My window is in blackout mode to keep the morning sun out. The only light in the room is a low green glow from my cathode ray desktop monitor. That small glow is plenty for me to find my bed as I plop in and sigh a thief's relief.

Chapter 5

Due to the nighttime nature of cryptid hunting, I have become nocturnal. Sleeping while the hiders tag beasts for migration pattern studies or radiation reading tests, by the time I wake up, this place is almost always a ghost town. Seekers like myself are awake, all but forcing the kitchen staff to make breakfast food all day 'round. Nothing but knee-high tea lights illuminate the halls. The blinding fluorescent lights in the cafeteria wake you up harsher than a bucket of cold water, but that sawmill gravy they keep on tap is worth every splash.

You can't hide from the buttery baking smell the second you enter through those cafeteria double doors. The sound of bacon sizzling in the back beckons you closer until the scent of the frying fatty meat has you positively salivating. A cup of black breakfast blend coffee is the perfect dance partner for the battle of the sweet gravy-covered biscuit and the savory, chewy bacon.

Sliding onto the bench seated tables with more anticipation than a first date, my fork flirts with every inch of my food tray,

CHAPTER 5

not knowing where to even begin revealing her. A quick rinse of coffee on my lips gives me time to decide. Bean companies always try to sell you on the 'rich nutty flavors' or 'caramel undertones with caramel overtones,' but that's all marketing; black coffee is black coffee. That bitter taste cleanses my pallet as I finally decide to get a hardy scoop of gravy-covered biscuit. It's not true for all, but it certainly is for me that this is the single most important feast of the day.

The cafeteria is never empty. Not surprising, seeing as there are a couple hundred people in this building at any given time. But, I keep my distance from my peers. All seekers are a bit reserved to themselves, but even still, my reclusiveness might be an outlier case. My stomach finally decides it doesn't have to eat itself for survival, and I look around to see who is joining me for the best meal of my life — until tomorrow's best meal of my life. Two seekers, the lovebirds Ann and Teddy, sit elbow to elbow on the opposite side of the benches a few tables over.

As I gnaw on this rubbery bacon, the great moth's words are gnawing at my subconscious. All day, I dreamed of that encounter. Flashes of his sharp teeth, his crooked smile, his hidden messages, the dream felt closer to a nightmare, but that is commonplace for me. To appease the nagging thoughts, I decide to do something out of character and socialize. Looking over at Ann, I stare till we make eye contact. I raise my hand to wave, and she replies with the same gesture, albeit with confusion painted from her raised brow to her curled lip.

"Good night, you guys." I cut the air like a rusty knife cuts raw meat.

Teddy joins Ann in her confusion but calls out back to me, "Hey, good night, Eric. Is everything okay?"

I know that I'm a recluse, and I know that I usually take my breakfast in my room, but asking if I'm *okay* just because I greeted them is still a little steeper than I expected. Telling them that everything is fine and about how much I'm enjoying my breakfast, I ask if I could join them to talk about some recent hunts they've been on. They seemed downright excited that I wanted to talk and waved me over with smiles.

Before I sit down with them, I offer to refill their coffees. Politeness can go a long way when you're trying to get people to open up to you. They reject my offer and usher me to sit across from Teddy.

Ann says that her last hunt was about five nights ago. She was sent to investigate a report of *Viridi cobolorum* — or green goblin — that was seen riffling through the trash. Teddy's last mission was a week ago tonight. He was sent to find a possible *Daemonium canis* — or chupacabra — that turned out to be a false alarm. One of the rare instances that, indeed, it was just an emaciated dog. For the record, we do take them in and treat them even though they are not cryptid in origin. Teddy says the little guy had some mange that needed tending and desperately needed a good meal but is doing much better now.

Ann's report, however, turned out to be real. She told me how an older woman was home alone and called our animal control number, saying a raccoon or an owl was harassing her. Seeing as raccoons are staunchly different from owls and vice versa, Ann was sent primed with a net launcher, knowing something needed to be caught. The old lady had said something was in her galvanized trash can making 'one heck of a racket,' and when she went to shew the creature away, it seemed to laugh as it chased her back inside. Poor lady, goblins are scary-looking buggers, but they are nearly harmless, albeit very mischievous. Ann said the cleaners offered the woman a new trash can and

CHAPTER 5

made her believe it was a gray barn owl that got a little territorial after being attracted to the shiny metal bin.

Sharing stories with the two is a better time than I intended. I never thought I'd find myself smiling this much at breakfast unless I was smiling at a fresh batch of sourdough waffles. My grandmother always said that robbing others of access to me would only hurt me in the long run. Isn't it weird how our brain chooses to remind us of things? Here I am, laughing at goblins messing with senior citizens and feeling hopeful pride hearing about the 'chupacabra' we are restoring to health. All these years I could've had this experience but instead, I scurried to my room like a rat that managed to steal the cheese from the trap. As much as I love being distant and oh-so mysterious, it is nice to let down my guard for once.

When I tell them about my seemingly much more dangerous recent hunt, they all but applaud me. Ann says she would never knowingly pursue a bigfoot without backup, to which Teddy, of course, assured her that he would always be one radio buzz away if she needed him. They make butterfly kisses that bring me back to hating social interaction. Ann hunted only a few days ago, Teddy a week, and I last night. Doesn't seem like there's exactly too much work to be done.

I try to peel back another layer of their trust and ask, "Do hunts seem to be getting more frequent for you guys?"

"Honestly, it's felt like a bit of a slow season," Teddy replies as Ann nods in agreement. "I wonder if the cryptids are finally learning about boundaries."

It's not like I can outright say, "Well, a mothman told me there are more missing monsters than ever." Making my best moth impression, however, I try to see what they think about a large exodus of beasts and what that could mean.

41

"Yeah, it's been business as usual for me too," I say. "But if we were busier, if we had more to hunt, what do you think would cause that?"

Ann and Teddy lock eyes like neither one of them knows what to say. Finally, Ann breaks the stare and says, "Every known pass from the Spikes to the Green is watched by us already. If there were more beasts, then there would have to be a new way for them to get here."

Teddy tacks on, "Oh yeah, maybe an earthquake could have opened a new rift in the rocks. Or maybe a thunderbird has started a trolley system where they carry paying customers over the rocky wall."

Ann shakes her head at the answers only a dude could come up with. She looks back at me and has a question of her own. "Are you thinking we're about to have an uptick in hunts? Your mom gave you some insider trading information?"

"Hardly," I answer with a deflecting chuckle. "Mom would sooner board that thunderbird trolley before telling me anything juicy."

We share a few laughs as Teddy doubles down on his amazing economic opportunity for large-winged creatures.

"It's unusual for there to be only one goblin, right?" I ask Ann. "Did you guys only find the lone ranger?"

"That's a good point now that I think about it," she says. "We only found one. The old lady had only reported one. Strange, but it is cryptids we're talking about. They are strange by default."

I shake my head in agreement with her. At this point, nearly half an hour had gone by, and I didn't want to keep them any longer, never mind that my social battery was nearing its end. Thanking them for their company and stories, I get up and make my way out of the cafeteria. Just as I am leaving breakfast, Mom

CHAPTER 5

is on her way in for dinner.

"There you are," Mom says. "I checked your room, but you didn't answer. I'm grabbing a to-go box, and I need you to meet me in my lab."

It's rare that a lab ever *needs* me. It could be some new tech she wants to show me, though, and I do love new tech, as chunky and faulty as prototypes may be. I agree to meet her, and she says to go ahead while she decides on her dinner plans.

After taking the elevator down to minus-one, it seems that most people have gone home for the night. Some enclosures I pass have cryptids of various breeds resting or eating or even one goblin playing with his dinner tray. Maybe that's Ann's goblin, I wonder. I don't see Teddy's dog friend; maybe he's asleep and hiding in one of these holding cells, or he's already roaming the streets again.

"Dr. Nguyen, Dr. Bush, Dr. Gamino, and last but not least, Dr. Grace Carpenter," I say to myself as I walk down the rows of private lab doors until I reach Mom's. Knowing I've got a few minutes for her to fill that to-go box to its brim, I lean to rest my shoulder on the door to Mom's lab. To my surprise, it doesn't hold my weight. Instead, the door swings open. Dr. Mom has left her office unlocked. This truly is a night of firsts.

There's a shuffling noise inside. She didn't leave it open. Someone opened it. The lights are off, but a flashlight's beam is dancing across Mom's desk. I've caught a legendary cryptid red-handed, a snooper.

Chapter 6

This poor guy thought he would be alone and have plenty of time down here. Leave it to a seeker to find you out when they're not even looking for you. A piece of me is jealous. I've never gotten to be in this lab unsupervised. There's no telling what he might be finding or trying to find. I'm supposed to be here, but he's not, so why do I feel nervous about calling out to him? I hate when people do things out of the ordinary. Can't we all just stay stuck in our ruts and wave as we pass each other by?

"He—Hello," I stammer. "What are you doin' in here?"

The light flashes off, and they make a half-measured attempt at ducking down. Something corrects their behavior, and they stand up tall. It looks like Dr. Hyde. Why would he be in Mom's lab?

"Dr. Hyde?" I call out. "That you?"

"Yes, ah, you caught me," he says, shaking his fist at me with a fake dismissive laugh. "Someone taught you too well."

I'd recognize his unkempt gray hair from anywhere. There are a million posters of him throughout this place. The worse

CHAPTER 6

his condition gets, though, the more his shoulders slump. He seemingly always keeps one hand in his lab coat pocket to keep his handkerchief in reach at all times.

"Are you looking for somethin'?" I ask him. "Mom should be down in a minute if you need her to—"

"No, no, no," he says. "She was working on something for me today, and I thought she had gone home without getting it to me. I was seeing if it was in plain sight."

Yeah, he's lying to me. Then again, he is her boss, and this is a relatively secret operation. Maybe he is looking for something, but he can't tell me anything specific.

"Find anything good?" I ask.

He grins, "About time your dog got an upgrade, huh?" He holds up a manila folder and raises an eyebrow.

"Shut up. Are you being for real?" I ask.

I flick the blinding overhead lights on and shuffle behind the desk with him. He thumps the folder and begins to speak, but a cough interrupts him. A bloody, speckled handkerchief raises to cover his mouth. Mom said he was sick, but not 'bleed out your esophagus' sick.

"What shall it be," he asks, "retracting claws or infrared night vision?"

"Claws, definitely claws." I lean in closer till my chin is hovering above his shoulder.

He recoils, closes the folder, and says, "If you blab about all this stuff, she will know I was here. It's our secret, right?"

He's a sickly old man who can't have much life ahead of him. The thrill of pilfering through his protege's research is probably one of his last acts of rebellion.

"Sure," my reluctance to agree gives way to my desire to see a new and improved Goigor.

45

He lays several schematics on the table in front of us. These aren't early development plans. These are blueprints. They, being someone smarter than me, could make these ideas a reality any day now. What's the holdup? Better question: why wasn't the cryptid-hunting robot dog given night vision in the first place?

Dr. Hyde is a smart man, and I've known him for as long as I can remember. I've never really felt close to him; he's like a distant cousin who's a little older than you. You know of him, but you don't know him. More accurately, he might be more like the rich uncle everyone has, but only ever hears about him in stories. He's too well off to be worried about family reunions, but he always sends a honey ham to show he didn't forget about the little people entirely.

There's more in this folder than metal canine parts. He slides a blueprint out of the way to reveal another. This one shows a remote control car. It's small, but Dr. Hyde says the idea is a small EMP burst set off by the car's onboard battery. Another blueprint uncovers from the shuffle. It looks like an upgrade to the rad suits. Dr. Hyde explains the current models are prone to tears around joints with a lot of movement. I could see why that would not be ideal for a suit designed to save the wearer from life-altering nuclear particles and why he, of all people, would want that suit as foolproof as possible.

A red corner hangs out of the stack of otherwise blue papers. While the doctor rambles about some insane fly swatter, I tug at the corner to reveal its design. It looks like an egg of some sort. The dimensions, if I'm reading this right, are about a meter in height. Is it an egg or an incubator for eggs? It's hard to tell. I'm not an engineer; I just know a bunch of them.

Hyde falls silent and places a hand on my shoulder. "You

CHAPTER 6

probably were not meant to see this one," he says.

"What do you mean?" I ask. "What is it?"

He palms his chin and gives the scruff on his face a comb with his fingers. "An incubation chamber of sorts. A chrysalis, really."

"Like a cocoon? What the hell is it for?"

"Funny you should gravitate to this," he begins. "It's not—"

"Ahem," sarcastic intrusion cracks from the door. "Can I help you boys with something?"

The jig is up. Dr. Hyde seems a bit panicked as he shuffles his folder back together. It's just a bunch of weird doohickeys. Are they actually supposed to be secret?

"The boy was outside your office waiting for you," Dr. Hyde says. "He said you were filling a carryout plate. I knew that would take some time, so I pitied him and let him inside."

Not a bad liar. Let's see if she buys it.

"I haven't forgotten about those readings you wanted if that's what you're snooping for," she answers.

She indeed did not buy it.

"I'd rather not discuss it in front of your boy," he says. His tone was a little sharper than it had been with me.

He squeezes by me to exit the room without a word. He and Mom exchange a glare. The mischievous feeling I had moments ago is now starting to feel like shame. Did he just use me to steal something and cover his tracks? Old shithead, I never liked him anyways.

"What was he looking through?" Mom asks.

"I don't know, a buncha blueprints of new tech."

"*Blue*prints?" she emphasizes.

"Yes, *blue*prints," I lie by omitting.

She sighs and steps around me to take a seat at her desk. Her

47

compostable to-go box squeaks open, and the sweet smell of baked apples and country-fried steak floats to my nose like a siren song floats to a sailor's ears. I can't be hungry again. Can I?

She takes a messy first bite, wipes her mouth with her thumb, and motions for me to grab a paper towel for her. She cleans her hand and points at a paper on her workbench. Instructions would be clearer if she took a breath between bites and used her words. I point at the page, and she nods. It looks like a list — a supply request form.

"What's all this?" I ask.

She swallows a gulp of fried chuck and says, "That's what I was gonna ask you. Geiger put a request in for all of that."

Damn it, G. So much for sneaking off between hunts. What's even on here? Rucksacks, a metal pot, protein bars, a flashlight, a silent scooter, and the list goes on. Sheesh, everything that ain't nailed down.

"Oh, yeah. We were thinking about a little camping trip," is the best lie I can come up with on such short notice. "I didn't know she was putting in this order, though. I would've proofread it. We probably don't need THAT much toilet paper."

"Camping?" Mom asks. "Since when do you camp?"

When was the last time I went camping?

"Me and Dad used to go all the time," I say without thinking. "Long, long, time ago. I guess most kids go camping, though, and outgrow it."

"He was a great outdoorsman," Mom says, resting her elbows on the desk to take a break from chowing down.

She stares off a bit, and the room gets quiet. We never talk about him. I knew better than to bring him up, but maybe this would stop her from asking too many more questions about our *trip.* There's always an awkward push and pull when someone dies unexpectedly. If you talk about them, you have to relive the pain. If you don't talk about them, you have to suffer the pain alone, all inside your head. For me, that's a dangerous place to be.

A lot of that day, I've forgotten. Whether it was for trauma reasons or lack of frontal lobe development at 6 years old, either way, it's all like glimpses through a porthole that's closing more and more each day. Sometimes, I still have dreams, but Mom doesn't want to hear about them. She prefers the 'never talking about him' route.

We all process grief differently. I just wish his death didn't also feel like a secret we had to keep. This place and its secrets make you forget what's public knowledge and what's a playing card that would topple the whole house.

"When are you two headed out?" Mom cuts through the thick air. "Or three? Should I check Molly's PTO schedule?" Her smirk betrays her and turns into a full smile. She's too proud of that one.

"And on that note, I bid you good night, madame."

"She's a good girl. Moms know these things sometimes, and I know she likes you."

"You know how you tell a kid that fire's hot, but they don't believe you till they wave their hand over the flame?" I ask.

She dismisses my analogy with her hands, making a shewing motion.

"It's a whole lot like that," I continue.

"You can't be a loner your whole life," Mom says. "Someday, you'll want to let the right people in. One day, you'll have someone that you'd do anything to keep. And you'll wonder how you ever got along without them."

"You're so right," I say. "Welcome to the Hyde Foundation, the perfect place to start a family. We've got single living spaces, a cafeteria, and community bathrooms. Everything downstairs must remain top secret, and the ping pong table never has a paddle with grip on the face. The perfect place to call home."

I look up at Mom, expecting her usual laugh or eye roll, but there is neither. She's looking down at her food, which has become a mound of cold playthings for her fork to endlessly bury and dig. Shit. What did I say?

"It's probably not ideal to start a family here," she begins, "but some of us had next to no choice."

"Mom, I didn't mean that. I was just—"

"It's fine. This place is practically all you know. That's mostly my fault, but we are safe here. After the attack..." she trails off, "it was just easier to be here than anywhere else."

I'm not sure if she's waiting for me to speak or if I should keep my mouth shut. I decide to jump in anyway. "The old house didn't feel right without him there," I say. "I don't blame you. And I was kidding about the pong paddles. The missing grip thing only happened once."

That got me a raised eyebrow and a pinched mouth corner out of her. I'll take that as a mild de-escalation.

"Do you remember enough of what your dad taught you to survive a whole weekend with just you and G?" she asks.

I walk around behind her chair and give her a lazy hug with my forearm across her chest. "I think so, one way to find out."

She grabs my elbow at its bend. "Trust yourself. You've always had a survivor's instinct. Trust it, too." After a couple of squeezes, she lets my arm go, and I head to the door. I'm stopped in my tracks at the frame when Mom calls out to me again. "I know you have questions about it all. And I'm sorry

I've never given you answers. Some days, I feel like I'm still processing it all, even decades later."

"You think it's any better for me?" I let slip out. When I look back at her, her eyes are down, and her hands are folded over one another with her elbows resting on the table.

Mom exhales. "No. I don't think that. I think the opposite." She lets her napkin drop to the table, landing on her mound of scraps. "It's not the easiest thing in the world for me to face you about."

"Clearly," I interrupt her.

Her lip quivers. She feigns wiping her mouth with the back of her hand to try and hide it from me. "I loved him too," she says. "I know you think I didn't and that I want to pretend like it never happened, but that's not true, Eric. It's just not true."

"Then what is true? Everything they hide, why let them hide him?"

I know what the papers said about the tragedy. I also know the hiders invented that story for the papers. They even cleaned up the mess under a circus tent so reporters couldn't see the full scale of the damage. It's bad enough to lose somebody. It's worse to have to keep a lie about the whole thing. I get it; we protect cryptids. But on that day, it felt like it came at the expense of us humans. Doesn't that defeat our purpose?

"I couldn't save him. But I saved you," her voice cracks. "That's how I choose to remember it. Not the day we lost him, but the day I saved you." Her palms push in on her eyes as she inhales to fight back tears. She lowers her hands and blinks ferociously at the ceiling.

"I'm sorry, Mom," I apologize. Seeing her cry plummets my heart. It's a visual reminder that I am and always will be an asshole. Dad wouldn't want us fighting. And he definitely wouldn't want me talking to her like this. "I'm outta your hair for a few days. See ya soon, okay?"

I hate stirring her up and then leaving her to put herself back together, but I'm not good at this emotional shit. If it was me, I'd want to be left alone, so that's what I do. I kick up dust and storm out. It's not fair for me to be this way. That's why I don't let anyone get in too close. They'd join in on my self-loathing sooner or later. I doubt Mom would even keep me around if I wasn't her own flesh and blood.

She says she loves me, and I half-heartedly wave goodnight to her. It won't be a good night, though. I ruined hers, and the thought of that ruins mine.

7

Chapter 7

Autumn turns any biome into a desert, with sweltering dry days and deathly chilling nights. Constructing an outfit of comfort for such a time is no easy task. This night, and most others, I am made of running shoes, athletic shorts, and an oversized hoodie — the usual preamble suit-up for my laps around the track.

Come winter, I'll be banished to the indoor milling treads, which I despise. I'm not seeking to burn calories like a hamster on a wheel. I am seeking a peaceful moonlit walk. Nothing helps me more than allowing my body to move itself for miles while my mind travels galaxies. A quick look at the stars reminds me of the minuteness of my problems, my anxieties, and my uncertainties.

Tonight, the sky is clear, and the moon is high. White light pours out of the large gym windows, illuminating the track outside. Not a soul fills the gym, and not a soul is out here with me, either. I'm grateful they never added blinding overhead lights around the track. They probably never figured anyone would be walking in the dark. Even on a determined path like this, stepping where you cannot see is dangerous. The light pollution from buzzing bulbs would cloud the sky and mute the stars that I love to see. The stars distract me from myself, from the spiral of thoughts and worry.

Am I blindly following the mothman into a death trap? Was what he said about cryptid disappearances even true? No one here strikes me as aware of any exorbitant exodus of mystery monsters. If anyone knew about such a subject, it would be us. Why would the moth make such an effort to find me just to lie to me? And if he wanted me dead, he could've just let the sasquatch do it or taken matters into his own prolegs.

My thoughts only ever lead to more thoughts, never a resolution. Half the time, I think things are out of my control anyway, and what happens kinda just happens regardless of our interest or intent. If I die beyond the Spikes, doesn't that mean it was destined to happen? And if I live, then isn't that fate as well?

The rubber track doesn't stand a chance at absorbing the clanks of Geiger's leaden feet. I can hear her from a mile away. Well, the track's only a quarter-mile in full length, but the sentiment remains. When she catches up to me, she raises up on her hind legs to walk in a more even cadence to mine.

"Physical exercise is great for the body, mind, and soul," she says. "I do not have a soul."

Why is she like this? "You are so weird," I point out to her.

"Weird is the way I am wired," she points out to me. "Are you ready for our journey tomorrow?"

I throw my hood over my head as I look around and make a dampening motion with my hands. "Shhh! That is a secret, remember?"

"Calculating," she says. "We are on an athletic track, in 42-degree Fahrenheit weather, at 0400 hours. Risk of compromising mission *Dirty Butterfly* assesses to '*MINIMAL.*'"

Smart-ass. "Yes, I'm ready," I say. "I mean, as ready as I can be. Have you done a little *risk assessment* on our trip?"

"I have. Several times. In order to avoid your retreat, I will not share the results."

"That tells me all I need to know. Thank you."

"We must make this journey," she says.

"I know why I wanna go, but what dog do you have in the fight? Other than yourself."

Her walking pauses as she pulls in a paw to cover the charging port on her chest — the equivalent of a heart. As her internal jukebox searches and statically plays a patriotic melody, she says, "I belong to the Hyde Research Foundation. Our goal is to ensure the safety of our world from cryptid creatures. If the moth warned of escaping anomalies, we cannot allow such things to continue."

My eyes rolled as soon as she started with that corporate crap. "A very regal answer," I say. "Now, why do you really wanna go?"

The plastic sliders that operate as her eyelids creep up to cover the bottom half of her pupils. The music scratches to a halt while her paws rub together in mischief. "It sounds too fun not to go; we must, Eric. We must!"

My head shakes as a source of disbelief as I flash my palms at her and continue my walk. "It could be dangerous. No, it *will* be dangerous," I remind her. "So, so, so dangerous. No one ever travels there. Not even us — the crazy people who research the other side. Don't you think we should at least *consider* not going?"

Her speedy two-legged walk is too insane. I can't watch her catch up to me because I would burst out laughing and ruin the

55

moment.

"Danger is inherent to our cause," she argues. "What mission have we been tasked that incurred no danger?"

"The usual danger is exactly that: usual," I retort. "We have no idea what we are walking into out there."

"I have taken precautionary measures in our supply order. As well as stolen a rad suit for you."

My face snaps down to her like a scolding mother ready to dole out punishment.

"I mean, of course, I procured a rad suit. Inconspicuously," she walks back her previous admission of theft.

"The worst-case scenario is I die," I remind her. "No offense, but they can rebuild you. Not me."

Her rubbery clangs fall behind me. When I investigate, her face hangs long like a child who just missed the ice cream truck and has to listen to its song dance into the horizon.

"They certainly can repair me," she says. "However, there is no circumstance even calculable in my memory that would ever require you to be repaired." I try to interrupt her, but she continues. "I would sooner never be restored from complete demolition than to suffer a moment of your discomfort. If any harm comes to you, friend, then I have failed us all."

I rest my arm around her shoulder and scratch her head. One thing the two of us have in common is worry. Some people have no one to worry about and no one that worries about them. If there's anyone I will never envy, it is such people.

Stern, as I try to be with her, I hope that she will protect herself more. With me, she's the opposite. She often wants to push me beyond my limits and get me out of my cozy state of rest. For our own reasons, we both want to go beyond the Spikes. As much as I want to deny it, we have to go. After a few silent laps of being nothing more than a boy and his dog, we head inside as the sky paints itself orange.

Chapter 8

As long as this place has been my home, it's never felt like one. Even in the cold months with heaters on full blast, these sterilized, blinding halls feel crisp. A home is supposed to be warm and inviting. The only warmth I feel here is from the showers and their rainfall heads. Speaking of, I think I'll run the whole building out of hot water before I climb into bed. Turning the latrine into a sauna and stopping by the cafeteria for a hot tea is all part of optimizing my bedtime routine to actually be able to sleep with the millions of thoughts wanting to pry my eyes away from rest.

We try to avoid the morning rush of early bird hiders by using the old dusty staircase to climb to our floor. Every step taken echoes up and down to every landing. Trudging up several flights is not ideal after sweaty miles of wandering on the track, but it avoids a dozen unnecessary half-smiles and half-hearted, "How are ya's?", so it's ideal to me. My steps are slower the higher up we get, but Geiger's energy never seems to run out. She has long forgotten the solemn silence we shared on the track.

CHAPTER 8

"Should we retrieve our traveling materials now?" she asks, standing at eye level and several steps ahead of me.

"We don't leave till tonight. Let's cross bridges when we get to 'em."

"I hate heights. There will be no bridge crossing unless positively mandatory."

Before I can explain my use of figurative language to her literal processors, we notice Dr. Hyde enter a double door on the floor above us. Twice in one night we have caught the old man looking over his shoulder. Either I am crazy or misremembering, but I swear I never see him twice in as many weeks, let alone one night. He looks up a flight, then down, but doesn't notice us as we are rounding the bend below, and he wheels in a cage.

"Dr. Hyde," I call up, "need some help?"

His shoulders jump, and he scans the corridor up and down again. When he sees me, his face turns redder than the sky of our new morning.

"Of course, it would be you," I hear his whisper bounce off the walls of this empty space.

"Sorry, what was that?" I call up to him.

His expression shifts in front of my eyes. "Perfect, it's you," he lies. "Help me with this, would you?"

Geiger and I quicken our pace to get to his level.

"CS-43981," Geiger reads aloud the label on the cage. "Jackalope specimen. Received 3 days ago. Physical test: '*PASSED.*' Survival assessment: '*YOUNG — RELEASE WITH LIKE SPECIES.*'"

"That's enough!" snaps the doctor. "Help me, won't you?"

"Sure," I say in an attempt to lower the weirdly high tensions. "Why are you moving a rolling cage via staircase anyways?"

Dr. Hyde's eyes dart from Geiger to me and back again. He

straightens his glasses and tucks a hand into his white coat pocket.

"Forgive me," he says. "It's been a long night, and now the morning crew is here, and the elevators are packed," he pauses for a breath. "Could you please help me get this to my office? I would owe you one, each of you, owe you two as it were."

Geiger and I exchange a look. I break first with a shrug. Grabbing the opposite end of the cage, I crabwalk my way backward up a flight, allowing no room between my legs for the cage to smack my shins. The jackalope inside is out cold, likely sleeping. The poor thing barely has little velvet nubs where its antlers will one day be. G did say it was young, and growing cryptids need their sleep. Once on his desired floor, we set the cage back on its wheels. With a nod, I hold the double doors open for the doctor, and he goes on his way. Geiger peers her head through the slit of the swinging doors.

"Strange, is it not?" she asks.

"Very. But he does own the place. Think he wants it as a pet?"

"Strictly against protocol. He should know. He wrote it."

"Think we should tell someone?" I ask.

"Dr. Carpenter, if anyone," she replies. "No one else."

"Sounds like a 'no' to me. I'm sure he has his reasons. Come on, we need shut-eye."

Continuing up the steps to the living quarters, I do not hear metal feet behind me. When I look, Geiger is standing at the double doors, still watching him through the crack.

"Are we doing something about it or not? It's your call," I tell her, giving her the final say.

"On any night that was not this night. You need rest," she says.

She trots to catch up to me and leaves the door gently

CHAPTER 8

swinging to a close. We reach our floor and stop by my room for a change of clothes. Well, change of clothes for me; Geiger stays behind and nestles into her charging bed. The color of lightning softly pulses from her joints as her battery is being refilled. I wish falling asleep were that easy for me. The only thing I fall into easily is nightmares. The ones that startle you awake in a way that you only ever see in movies and surprise you with their realness when it happens to you for the first time.

I couldn't even enjoy my shower. The water burned so hot my skin turned red, but I liked it. I stood in the rainfall until the hot spring water turned glacial. There were no thoughts in particular on my mind. Something was in the way.

Every day before a mission is a sleepless one. That anxious anticipation turns every page in my mind like it's a newspaper stand caught in a thunderstorm. There's something about the words from that moth that I can't get out of my head. He questioned who I was and what I could do, and then he summoned me to the Spikes. What was it for? Does he really need me, or does he intend to use me, just as the Hyders do now?

The nerves welling up inside me either won't let me sleep or will jolt me awake in a sweaty, nightmare-fueled heap in an hour or so. Stress and trauma are the leading causes of recurring nightmares, and my brain seems to have a favorite visage it loves to visit.

Every time, the dream is the same. A sunny spring morning heading in through the giant oaken doorway of the church house. There are two steps that lead up to the door, the frame of which has bird nests on either upper side. Mom has me by one hand, and Dad has me by the other. The church feels massive, with vaulted ceilings that are at least ten times my height. The sun shines in every hue of the rainbow through the stained glass windows that line the back and two side walls. Each window depicts its own story in a single image; one shows a dove, one shows a cross, and another shows angel wings.

At the front is the pulpit, behind it is a giant baptismal tub whose water is capable of coming out of the tap at near boiling temperature, or at least that's how it felt to a young boys skin. The wall above the tub has a beautiful creek view mural painted on it as if the members needed a reminder of how gorgeous nature can be. They only need to look outside to know that truth. This church rests far at the end of the Green in a quaint community a few country miles north of the Spikes.

The building's floor creaks beneath Dad's feet as this country wooden church reminds the congregation of its many years of service. Generations of families have come here every Sunday, a small loyal following proving itself to be greater than a larger, more hollow group. Dad loves this old place. Mom, however, is more of the holiday-only type of church goer.

The weathered pews roar with each and every shift of weight forced upon them. The pews, the floor, the bell hanging high in the steeple; everything within these walls seems to sing out. My favorite part of church was, in fact, the singing. In the spring, the first choir I would hear was always the birds outside chirping for joy in the defrosting sunlight. The next choir was the aged wood telling tales of its wisdom. The last choir, of course, was *the* choir that sat up on stage in front of the tub and mural. In spring, only the most jubilant and happy, hopeful hymns were sung. This time of year was for boundless life and growth. The winter cold had gone and taken everyone's depression with it.

There was this one hymn that I loved to hear Dad sing. His voice could reach the deepest bass, making the surrounding

CHAPTER 8

rows of vocalists turn to see where such a note could be coming from. The hymn always reached a striking point where the music paused, and with all the might my little voice could muster, I'd shout:

Up from the grave he arooose! With a mighty triumph o'er his foooes!

The congregation, all in unison like a crashing wave, could make the floor of this old-fashioned building shake to its studs. None more so mighty than my dad. When he sang out that resounding first word, 'Up,' the heavens themselves heard it. It made your heart nearly leap, and your hair felt like it conducted current. The preacher would joke about the choir singing so good that the stained glass panes were vibrating. He meant it, of course, as hyperbole, but on that day, the windows actually began to shake.

The shaking turned quickly to spiderweb-shaped cracking. The cracking turned into a full-on implosion of the stained glass. Shards of red, blue, and white flew inward, shattering all across the people in their finest linens. Everyone fell silent at once. Even the whistles of the songbirds had gone missing. A moment of shock and deafening silence was then replaced with a horrid, wrenching, bestial scream. Bursting in from the window seal that once held a colorful glass creation of a dove and olive branch was a screeching *Volantem mortem* — flying death — it was an ahool.

Ahool are as violent as cranky apes with twice the size and strength. Their faces are stuck in a snarl reserved only for cornered chimps. Compounded by their ability to take flight on overgrown bat wings, it is not common to encounter one that allows you to tell the story. Had it been one ahool, maybe that day would have turned out differently. Maybe we all worry at first, but the beast is intimidated when he sees how he is outnumbered by a crowd of humans.

Thudding resounds across the auditorium as the padding of ahool palms strike the roof and steeple. Another ahool crashes in through the beloved stained panes. As huge and as blaring as the ahool are, it was rare to see them in numbers greater than one. Doubt soon took over every believer's mind. People from the back pew to the front are all cramming for the exit through the single-file aisles. Children are screaming, the building is rattling, and the brass bell is clanging against its wooden tower. I grab Dad's hand and look up to him for answers, but as I do, I see a ceiling strut crashing down toward us from overhead.

The pack of ahool crumbled that ancient wooden structure. Flakes of white wooden shrapnel sticking out of the rubble with splintery jagged edges. Once they targeted our holy house with their aggression, it was too late. Whether it was a wooden beam or one of the many silver fixtures hanging above us, something fell and nearly crushed my head.

From that moment, I can recall only horrific still frames in my mind. I can see my mother's panicked eyes as blood begins to mix with her tearfully running makeup. I see the blue sky above and hear only heaving cries as the sound of collapsing wood grows more distant, then bright fluorescent bulbs on a tiled ceiling. After that, nothing. Nothing for what felt like a very long time.

When I wake, I see Mom in the world's most uncomfortable chair at the end of my bed with a leg resting over one of the armrests like she can't find a restful position. Her eyes are bloodshot, and her eyelids are raw. Her hair defines the messy

CHAPTER 8

bun, and she is wearing her long white work coat. When she noticed my eyes opening, I suppose neither of us had ever felt such massive weight removed from our shoulders. She held me so tight it was like I could feel her very heart trying to reach out and embrace mine. In that embrace, she wailed so loudly that I knew my burning question did not need to be asked: Where is Dad?

We never really talked about that day or about him. No matter his exact cause of death, dead is still dead. Growing up, when Mom had too much wine with her spaghetti, she might fall into a cursing mood and say with her face to the sky, "If Scott wasn't special enough to protect, then no one is special to you." Mom never took me back to church, even after the faithful congregation took Hyde's hush money and had the place rebuilt.

My dad would be ashamed of her, but if I said something like that to Mom, then he would be ashamed of me. So, this was the beginning of accepting. The beginning of never asking questions because asking questions would only be picking at scabs, never fully allowing anything to heal. Did the silence heal either of us, though? I never challenged what Mom said to be true about anything. Even if I disagreed and even if I knew Dad had taught me better, it was easier to nod than to fight.

He has been gone close to 20 years now, but every time I allow that frame of the slideshow to be viewed, I yank the chord from the wall. If I don't run from the thoughts, the grief overtakes my logic, and tears overtake my vision. Hearts don't mend like bones. And tears don't dry like blood. People only see the scars of wounds that heal. But the wounds that don't, you get to admire those all alone.

Maybe that's why the moth occupies my mind. He knew what he was seeking, and he pursued it. That guy is a mystery, but he's definitely a challenger. A beast coming through the Spikes for the purpose of finding a human — that simply is unheard of. I didn't even know they were smart enough to wear clothes; now, all of a sudden, a cryptid detective is showing up. Dad was similar, in a way. If he needed something or someone came knocking looking for him, he wasn't shy. He was bold.

Then there's me. Living in a buttoned-up bubble of a life, never stepping out of line. They covered up the ahool incident and lied about every detail to everybody who asked. I didn't take up for Dad. I let them lie in his name. Monsters killed him, but I've had to go around pretending the church had a structural failure that brought the whole place down. All for what? Keeping poachers from hunting the damned things. Maybe they should. This catch and release could be a carousel we never can get off of.

I can't think like that, I know. We are doing the right thing. Even if in the wrong way. My father would be ashamed, my mothman would be ashamed, but tomorrow, all of that ends. Tomorrow, the true seeking begins. We're going looking where we didn't even know things could be hiding. And we're not coming back with questions. We're coming back with answers.

9

Chapter 9

Before we can begin, we have to be supplied. My pointer finger nearly taps an indent on the supply room's front desk. I have been poking my head in and out of the service window, offering my voice as a guide to any workers lost in the storerooms behind this glass partition.

"Hellooo, am I the only one that does any work around here?" I call out for what feels like the hundredth time. "Useless," I say, shrugging toward Geiger.

"'*GARRETT*' works the supply room night shift," Geiger says, utilizing a tape of Garret's own voice saying his own name. "He is known all the building over for his punctuality and persnickety way of dealing. Supply opens nocturnally at 1700 hours, and with '*GARRETT*,' not a moment sooner."

"I'm sure. Hard to be fashionably late when you gel your hair into submission and give no thought to how many buttons are too many buttons to button on a button-up."

My foot attempts to snake its way into my mouth when my rant is interrupted by a cough that sounds like, "Ahem." My lifted eyebrows cannot hide my expression of guilt.

"Garret!" I say with life, trying to swallow my shame. "Is it 1700 already? Boy, time flies. Doesn't even feel like we've been waiting here for 13 and a half minutes."

He looks unimpressed with me as always, but he wipes his chagrin away with a push upward on the bridge of his glasses. "Good evening," he says. "I'm guessing you are retrieving the order Geiger placed?"

"Yes," I say, motioning down to her, "we are."

The supply man leans over the desk and looks at Geiger. "Ah, I almost didn't see you there." He sticks his head back inside and pulls a drawer open. After a few seconds of shuffling, his hand extends out of the window with a dog treat. He tosses it down to her, "We always love to be visited by our furry friends."

Geiger eyes the treat, then eyes me. She doesn't eat dog treats, being an android, but she also doesn't want to hurt his feelings. She cracks the spine of the femur-shaped cookie between her teeth, "Mmm, delectable."

Before I can cover my laugh, his hand extends out the window again. This time, he holds a blue band with black plastic clips on each end. "Don't forget to wear your collar when you leave the facility," Garret minds us. "Company policy."

Geiger's face mimics a queasy feeling. "Yes, of course. We will equip the collar as soon as we reach the edge of company property."

"Well, we don't wanna forget," I say to Geiger, hiding a smile behind my hand. "Maybe let's just do it right now."

She throws a venomous look at me. She hates collars, and she knows that I know she hates collars.

"Why do later what you can do right now?" Garret chimes in his support.

"Exactly," I say as I kneel down, my voice cracking in delight.

CHAPTER 9

Her puppy dog eyes try to silently talk me out of this cruel and unusual fate, but it *is* company policy, after all. The clip clasps in place with a plasticky pop around her neck. This popping noise might as well have been a 'play' button as Geiger softly raises the volume on a tape recording playing a sad violin melody. "Drama queen," I say with a tousle at her snout. "We'll take it off outside, promise."

"That's much better. Good girl, Geiger." Garrett's floating head says as it peers over our side of the service desk and drops down another treat for her. "Now, the rest of your request is here," he slides out a cardboard box that scrapes dust off the counter as it goes. "Keys to your scooter are here, and you can pick it up at the loading bay."

I've never seen this man out from behind the supply desk. For all I know, he could have 8 hairy, nasty spider legs below his waist. It's funny to hear him explain to me where I need to go to retrieve things. If I asked him for directions, I doubt he could even point us in the right Cardinal way.

"Thank you," I say as I snatch the box.

"These are items meant to be returned; they are not *yours*," Garret punctuates. "You have them rented for the next three days. They must be returned no later than 1800 hours on the third day. Should anything be lost or stolen, you are respon—" he drones on and on as my attention turns away and away.

"Rules, rules, and rules. I got it. See ya then," I interject.

My momentum is halted as he scoots a piece of paper out to me. "Please sign here, date here, and answer this one question at the bottom for me," he taps a pen down the page with each instruction.

"*What is the intended use of the items rented?*" I read aloud at Garrett. "That's new. They gettin' even more nosey around here?"

"Company policy," he shrugs. "They like to know where all company property goes and what it's being used for."

'*Top secret plan for world domination*,' I scribble down in the allotted text box. "Later," I toss at Garrett over my retreating shoulder.

He audibly tufts at my questionnaire but still offers a half-measured "Later" in return.

Me and the rule-compliant canine at my side make our way down to the loading bay. Geiger has the key ring to our scooter dangling from her mouth as a way to muzzle herself from nervously spilling any beans all over the garage floor. We walk to the end of the row of vehicles and locate our chariot. White plastic and black leather suspended on four wheels: two tightly tucked on the front and two tightly tucked but slightly larger in diameter on the back. Four wheels on a scooter add stability, hopefully, enough stability that this fifty-pound box of camping gear doesn't slide off the back cargo rack.

Geiger takes her seat on a leather bump above the back of my seat. The scooter is electric, so my attempts to rev it up and make a grand escape are silently whirring away just like we are.

It's a strange feeling, really, moving toward an event momentous for you that no one else even knows about. It's what I imagine proposing to your lover would be like. To everyone else, it's just another day, but to me, my palms could sweat a glove full, and my overthinking is a teeter-totter between amazing and horrendous outcomes. If all goes well, no one will ever know where I went, and if all goes not so well, still, no one will ever know where I went. This must be what a ghost feels like — still around, but it makes no difference.

We make a quick pit stop at the edge of the compound yard.

CHAPTER 9

Geiger buried my rad suit in a clump of leaves behind a giant tree trunk. That suit is gonna smell like clogged gutters, but stinking in the suit is better than microwaving my cells outside the suit. I hoist the dripping rubber into our cardboard box and begin to have some serious doubts about this whole thing. Before the thoughts can catch up to me, we are flying down the road as fast as a 2500-watt battery can carry us. The roads headed south are paved for a while, but the blacktop, as if regressing backward in time, slowly fades to stone, then gravel, which fades from dirt to barely padded grass.

We pass old country shacks and houses. This part of the Green has all but been abandoned as every child who grew up here dreamed of a larger life in the city. Once those dreamers were old enough to pursue, they spread their wings and flew far. Some families stayed here until the foliage on their heads drooped gray and the flowers on their graves blossomed high. Some couldn't stand the distance between themselves and their little birds, so they followed them to the city. All the same, you're not likely to meet someone out here. The occasional fisherman may be spotted heading from honeypot to cabin. Most life here is unkempt. The critters and the weeds grow at any pace they see fit. The world is in it's most natural state.

Abandoned homes might as well be tombs — reminders of life and life gone by, that is. The stories that once painted the walls have long been peeled. The happiness that once warmed the beds are now frigid, frayed sheets. The beam of the popup headlight coming from our steed brushes across a familiar mailbox. The breaks squeal us to a stop as Geiger and I sit in silence. It's not often that Geiger doesn't have anything to say, but I suppose neither of us has been at this address for more than a few moments since Dad passed.

"Would you like to go inside before we go further?" she asks.

"No," I say. "There's no one in there to say goodbye to."

Her paw rests on my back. I didn't expect her consoling touch. The sudden weight of it nearly makes me lose my grip on the precious tear I am fighting with. Knowing that I can't speak without revealing the true hurt of my heart, I turn the wheel south and point my mind toward the task at hand. Here or not, I know Dad is proud of us, his two kids, for going out of our way, way out of our way, to help cryptids. If we die for that choice, then so be it. I'll know we died making him proud, just like he did for us.

The night is dark, and nothing looks as it does in the day. Even places traveled a million times take a new shape in the moon's light. This area is so far south that I don't recognize a thing. In all my adventures and fake runaways, I never dared go this far.

The grass is burning out, and the ground below us looks like volcanic rock formed after an eruption. There is no volcano here. This slate is a sign that we are drawing nearer to the Spikes. Geiger's chest beeps about every thirty seconds now; the faster the beep, the closer we are to her marked coordinates. I'm afraid that if she turns on her rad counter, the two noises will overlap and drive me so insane that I crash the scooter on purpose. We will live in ignorant bliss of the radiation until we find whatever the moth is trying to show us.

Plant life has a hard time living here. Flora beyond the Spikes grows at an abounding rate and size. They are much like the plants on this side of the wall, only larger and more nutrient-hungry. There is a weird area around the wall where nothing grows. The life inside and the life outside never meet.

The rock formations of the spiked wall completely insulate

one side from the other. The rocky surface stretching below our wheels now is a barren and unlivable surface. All of this is logic in my head, facts taught to me in school. None of that explains the truth of what I am seeing before us now.

The lights of the scooter crawl their way up the Spikes; we have arrived. Geiger's beeping tells us that we are exactly where we're supposed to be. I cut the wheel to a stop and throw down our kickstand. We hop off the machine, and Geiger activates her brightest front-facing beam.

"Is that—?" I begin to ask.

Geiger cuts me off, "A gap in the Spikes."

A dark hole, a cavern, is set before us — a crag split open in the Spikes, but not just that. The outline of a great tree appears in our torchlight. Between the rockbound wall and the gateway to the hard place, a tree.

"A new gap or an unguarded one? Which is more likely?" I ask Geiger.

"If all openings were identified, then there would be no escapes," she says. "Perhaps we have discovered a new route. We can share the coordinates with reconnaissance when we return."

"*If* we return," I scoff. "Monsters can walk in and out of here as they please. They've got a freakin' runway. Something could walk out here and eat us at their leisure."

Geiger dims her light and doesn't scold me for my dramatic hyperbole. She simply says, "Then we had better get ready."

Chapter 10

Our journey from here must continue on foot. Our scooter may be a marvel of modern engineering, but it does not handle as well in bushy jungle terrain. I plop my duffel bag down to the ground and retrieve the rad suit. Geiger needs no such protection. Hell, she gives off her own minute amount of radiation, but me and anything else not born in the Rads, we'd be sour raisins in a few hours.

Rad suits were made to be completely insulated from harmful waves. The gill-like vents on the side of the body help circulate air out of the suit while a muzzle below the glass window filters air in. Breathing and not being microwaved is great and all, but I think we could've invested a few extra dollars into comfort and fit. Safe from the rads, but the chaffing — oh, the chaffing.

Squeaking with my first few steps in the new suit, I make sure our supplies are in order. It's hard to plan for a trip whose duration is unknown. Geiger has already expressed concern about teaching this moth the power of a thorough itinerary. For now, however, it's just me and her, a few gallons of water in camel packs, an emergency tarp top in case we need shelter,

CHAPTER 10

and a few bolas if things get weird — weirder than usual. We're ready to begin the hike, but this hole in the Spikes is still a point of worry.

"My feelings are almost always the good kind," Geiger reminds me, "but I am currently experiencing a sensation akin to caution."

"We're at the Spikes," I say. "Everything's gonna look creepy. Might as well get used to it now."

"Threats should be assessed. There could be anything beyond this wall," she pleads again.

"*Anything*. Exactly. *Anything* is an impossibility to know. When you figure out how to prepare for the impossible, we'll go right ahead and prepare. But until then, let's hurry up and get this over with." I say, trying to be stern to her. We can't end this before we even begin.

"There is one threat we can see," she says. "Let us assess it at the very least."

"The tree, G? The tree?" This claustrophobic neoprene is making me irritable. "Ya know what, good idea. I'll go assess your tree. Your cryptid tree."

I hear tapes swirling around inside her before she says, "Potential risks include but are not limited to '*FALLING LIMBS, EXPOSED ROOTS, PARASITIC INSECTS.*' Please approach with caution."

"Watch my head, watch my step, don't get a spider bite. Got it."

Though a radioactive spider bite sounds kind of fun, I saunter my way toward the *Ligna minas* — or timber menace — with careful steps. She was made to be the perfect assistant to seekers, but being leery of arboretums makes me think she must have a screw loose. Cryptids are animals; they're fauna.

Radiation certainly has the capability of getting creative with flora, but we study those things, too. Flytraps catching hummingbirds is weird, but if I can't take on overgrown crabgrass, we might as well get back on that bike and tuck our tails.

"Less than 12 meters out, sergeant," I radio back to Geiger with the walkie built into the suit's helmet. "If I don't make it back, tell the kitchen staff I love them."

"They are well aware. Act serious, please."

"Oh, I am serious," I say. "This is the spookiest tree I've ever seen. I mean, wow, just look at the leaves and the wood. Not just any tree can have that stuff, ya know."

"Eric, stop. What is that?"

"Sarcasm. I know figurative language sometimes trips you up, but I thought you were fluent in sarcasm."

"No," she says, ignoring me. "Above you. The shape from here reminds me of an athletic sneaker."

I look up, and she's right. Why is there a shoe hanging up in the branches? That thing is way up there, too. Who can even throw it that far?

"Another anomaly. Mind your peripherals," Geiger coaches me.

"You put this marshmallow-ass suit on and then talk to me about peripherals."

I have to turn my shoulders in the same direction as my head to check my left and right like I'm sealed into a neck brace. On the ground near my footing are bones. Not a pile, not a carcass. An assortment of bones. I backpedal to make sure I'm not walking on someone's unofficial burial site. When I do, I stumble. My heel tripping on an exposed root. I barely catch myself an inch off the ground, lucky not to have cracked the glass dome around my face on the root system.

CHAPTER 10

"Get up," Geiger demands. "Return to my location."

"Calm down, G. I'm fine. I didn't see that root there."

"It's because that root was not there. It moved to follow your steps."

Groaning bark is a noise found in nature, but hearing it so loudly feels otherworldly. The roots and branches are roughly contorting themselves. Vines and leaves are grasping at my hands. Son of a bitch, can't that dog ever be wrong about something. The ground begins to shake, making it hard for me to maintain any semblance of balance. It feels like an earthquake is spawning from the roots. The groaning of flexing wood is beginning to sound more like the pained moans of a phantom.

"Can I get a little help here?!" I plea to any ears that will listen.

Geiger is trying to bounce her way over to me, but it's not like she is immune to the crumbling earth. Searching around me for anything to brace with, unfortunately, the branches of the monster are all that I can reach. A branch is bent over my head, it's just barely in arms length.

I push myself up with all my strength, hoping that the reaction doesn't knock loose the ground below me. My hand grasps at the wooden support. First, it slips, but then I feel lighter. My grip must be tighter than I had thought. Both hands are now grabbing the branch, and I pull myself up. And up. And up.

Once feeling lighter, I now feel weightless. I swivel my head around, trying my best to see through the steamed mess of a glass pane on my face. The very vine I was reaching for had instead been reaching for me. Thorns dig into my ankle as the tight knot of the wispy branch has wrapped itself around my leg several times over. I am fully caught in this thing's snare, whatever this thing is.

"Geigeeer! Could use a hand here!"

Searching for her in the landslide of debris, I find that we are doomed to the same fate. She is hung up in another branch, snarling at any limb that dares get close. Our motion is in sync, me and G are raised closer together like a mother preparing to scold her fighting children.

There is a brief pause in the chaos, a brief moment of clear air, and we find ourselves staring at the thick trunk of this ancient arbor. A high whining noise begins to ring out. In the center of this massive trunk, a scar-like crack begins splitting open the bark. Once the sideways gash has reached its limit, a faint yellow glow, like a jack-o-lantern's candle, flickers light on our petrified expressions. This thing has an eye, and it's looking right through us.

The entire forest around us begins to shake, leaves falling, dirt crumbling. In a roar of wind or vibration of wood — hell, I don't know — somehow, this tree was speaking. The voice is hard to make out, even for me. It speaks like it is out of breath, but it needs no air. It speaks like its throat is dry, but it needs no water. The tree grumbles, on time like a metronome, echoing from the forest floor.

"*My bark has bite. My shade brings night. My eye gives light to savor your fright. A tree stays in place, but I keep pace. A forest of me, no quarter for thee. Your heart unsteady; I see you already. Your life, I claim, lest you speak my name.*"

This can't be happening. An evil tree is speaking in riddles for the fate of our lives, and we aren't even a hundred meters beyond the Spikes. Might as well meet our grim end now. I don't guess it would've gotten any easier from here.

CHAPTER 10

"That was fun, but I am leaking fluid," Geiger chirps. "Did you happen to understand those sensory-dampening wails?"

"He ain't telling nursery rhymes, that's for sure," I relay to her. "We either have to call him by name or be beaten into fertilizer."

The night breeze is rustling the creature's leaves, but otherwise, it is motionless.

"Can we have another hint here, asshole?" I ask. "It's not like you could guess one of our names after hearing us tell a poem."

Pretty sure my ankle's bleeding and this suit is a sauna, I'm skipping common courtesy.

"Are you sure '*ASSHOLE*' was a good first guess?" Geiger pries, using my own voice against me.

"Whether he eats us or lets us go, I wanna get there fast. None of those bones, the clothes, knew the answer, and that must be the point. The game is rigged." I gruff back at her.

"Less of a game and more of a trivia, it would seem," Geiger says.

The ground shakes again like an aftershock. I suspect we are being told to hurry up.

"What did the beast say, exactly?" she tacks on.

"I don't know, they said it once, and it sounded like wind blowing through a trumpet with a buncha gravel in it."

"Recite what you recall, please. Swiftly."

I close my eyes and send my brain into a blast before beginning. "'Shade like night,' 'watches your fright,' 'something something spaghetti, I can see you already.'"

"Stop!" Geiger commands. "'*SEE YOU ALREADY.*' That phrase is in my database. Searching and deciphering."

Another aftershock. A moment later, another. It's like we are being counted down.

Geiger continues, "Records of a carnivorous willow. Only stories, hard to verify sources."

"Name, a name," I spit at her. "Focus on a name. If this thing is an urban legend, what did they call it?" I was at peace with dying, but if we find the answer, we might as well live.

"No evidence of the beast. Only theory. Filtering local colloquial." Geiger sputters out information as she finds it.

The aftershocks are growing increasingly close together, almost like a drum beat now. The vines suspending us in the air are moving again. The creaking wood, followed by splintering bark, resounds. Below the eye opens a splintery abyss.

"Any minute now, G!" I beg her. But she remains silent, focusing on her task.

The grip of the thorny cordage is beginning to loosen. The beat of the roar cannot get any faster or any louder. A crashing chomp of jagged bark is my last warning for locking in my final answer. I look over to Geiger. The poor girl is still lost in her head. But it looks like I'm first on the menu anyway. At least this way, I won't have to watch her be turned into scrap; that's the only thing the tree could do to me that would be worse than death. I'm gonna close my eyes now and try to think about when trees were sentinels of protection instead of whatever the hell this monster is.

Being subsided to the thought of passing, the chaos is a little quieter. Everything sounds strange in this suit. Sound bounces off the plastic surface in a weird underwater-like echo. But for a second, it's all clear. I swear I can even hear a gust of wind approaching me right now. It almost sounds like words, but they have no meaning. "Ya-Te-Veo," the wind whispers to me.

"Ya-Te-Veo," I chuckle to myself. "Worst last words ever."

CHAPTER 10

My serenity gets too comfortable. It's like all tumult has ceased as I am being slowly lowered down to the mouth of the beast. The wood is creaking again, but my descent is slow and guided. I open my eyes to get a last look at this uncharted beast's gullet, but I'm not in a gullet. I'm on solid ground.

"Did you speak the cryptid's name? Splendid work!" Geiger cheers for me.

"I didn't — no. I don't know." Better than saying, 'The wind told me,' I suppose.

"What was it you said? Something was erased in my folklore archives. I was attempting to recover."

"Ya-Te-Veo. The wind told me to do it." So much for that secret.

"Speaking to the wind now? You must truly have a way with words." Geiger spins this, as she does everything, toward the positive light.

Our tree friend is shut up. No eye, no hole in the ground, roots appearing planted, like nothing ever happened. Someone had to have told me that answer, a nearby cryptid hiding out. But why? And who? If that damn moth pops up in a minute or two, that'll be one more mystery solved. Speaking of, maybe we should get out of this bog before Mr. Veo comes up with another riddle.

"We really should beat it before we accidentally trigger this guy's trap again. Which way we goin'?" I ask Geiger.

My answer does not come from her but from a high perch. "From here, the two of you should follow me."

In a tree branch above us is the fashionably late mothman. I toss criticism up to him as high as I can throw it, "Moths are always tardy to tragedies, right?"

"Welcome, seeker," the moth says. "Yatee is an old friend; I had thought he would remain dormant. It must have been the clamoring of your supplies mounted on the motorized scooter. It fits you very well," he tosses criticism back down.

"The Mothman! How nice to see you again, I think," Geiger never forgets her manners. "Eric, translate for me. I know he is happy to see us, too."

If you've ever left your dog at home for a few hours and come back to them jumping with joy to celebrate your return, that's Geiger with everyone and everything. She once bit a man who was snooping around my dad's fishing boat and then approached said man for pets at the grocery a week later.

She is an advanced AI with all the modern cassette tech they could squeeze into her little blocky chassis, but she is also very much a dog. She only remembers the good and pretends there was never any bad in the first place. My mother certainly designed her with me in mind. Mom knew I would need somebody quick to forgive and forget.

"In the spirit of *dear old Yatee*," I prod the bug, "why don't you tell us your name now? We've earned our fair share of trust." I cross my arms to give the impression of being tough and peeved. The squeaky and foggy radiation suit betrays my display.

"Forgive my lack of manners in our last meeting. It was quite hastened." He jumps down from his perch and lands in a crackling of sticks and crunching of leaves. "My name is Phorbas. You may call me as such. 'Friend' or 'brother' works just as well," he answers.

"Little early for 'friend,' little weird for 'brother'; Phorbas it is. Why did you drag us out here, Phorbas? You get off from watchin' monsters nearly eat people alive?"

He chortles a response, "I needed to see how you handled yourself. An adult man speaking to his supernatural captor like a troubled teen. It was, unfortunately, what I had expected. Nevertheless, your willingness to enter the Rads at all is quite heroic. A sculpture must be carved from a boulder and not a pebble, I suppose."

"Well, this boulder is pissed and a little piss-covered," I say at him, not to him. "This shit better be worth it, or we—"

The mothman tips his hat to me and stops my rant in its place, "My apologies in all their depths belong to you, brother. It was wrong of me to allow a foreign challenge in a foreign land." He rests his hat back on the crown of his head. "Do you see? How harsh words stir up wrath, but a soft answer turns away anger?"

That bastard. "You bastard. Don't high horse me."

"Just imparting," he says. "It could save you next time I'm not around to solve your riddles for you."

We go back and forth for a while; him with old wives sayings, me with calling him anything but a son of God. It was fun. He doesn't back down from me. For all intents and purposes, I think I trust the guy. But he's still a know-it-all smartass.

"Grab your packs. We have another friend of mine to meet," he says, turning on his heel spur and heading deeper into the forest.

"Now, wait just a second here," I object. "Your last friend almost turned us into mulch. Tell us exactly who we are expecting."

Over his trench-coated shoulder, he hollers back, "This friend is vegetarian. You are safe with me, brother."

So we're brothers now, great. Not that I've felt prepared for this trip even once, but I feel desperately out of my element here. Geiger still has her head in the clouds from all the excitement. I'm not gonna be able to convince her to turn back. I think we are on this journey for the long haul, even if that long haul kills us at the next stop.

The forest is quiet. Every once in a while, I hear scampers of little feet over leaves but never catch a glimpse of the critter. It's not like I expected to see families of jackalopes or packs of keelut, but I'm surprised how little of anything we have actually seen. Maybe Mr. Veo wards off most wildlife in these parts, or maybe cryptids are nearly as scarce on this side of the wall as they are on our side.

"Is it always this eerie?" I call ahead to Phorbas.

"This area is not so rife with life," he says. "Mostly scavengers and the mischievous sort."

"Do ya have communities? Cities? You're wearing a tailored suit, for cryin' out loud," I press him further.

He lets out another chilling chortle, "The suit was a gift, I'll have you know. It is fitted, but hardly tailored. But, yes, we do. *Some* do. There are varying degrees of..." he pauses like he's deciding on which word to use, "...consciousness."

"Is that where we're headed? A moth city?"

"Moths are more likely to call their dwelling place a village, but no. We are en route to a hub of sorts, where any manner of beast might reside," he explains. "Most rad dwellers are self-sufficient, though, as you will see, there are some exceptions."

Surprisingly, the forest doesn't last long. After wading through sticks and brush for the better part of dawn, we come to a cliffside. Being under the canopy of trees almost made me forget it was morning. The sun is revealing miles of an expansive treetop valley before us.

In the far distance is a rad storm cloud with a deep gray belly and lime tentacle lightning firing off every few seconds. I have never seen such a landscape nor such a storm. I can also finally see some life. A v-shape of birds flies heading away from the storm. We are so high up that we are at eye level with the unknown avian species in the distance.

Phorbas points forward at a small clearing in the valley ahead, "Behold, the town of Kelly."

I can't believe how much the view strikes me. It's not like a view you might get at the end of a long hike — sweaty, staring at plain treetops alongside a hundred of your closest friends, all fighting for the best photo. Everything is impossibly green, and every leaf is impossibly large. The radiation feeds everything. It takes the normal of our side and stacks it on top of each other to make something as typical as a tree seem almost alien. Almost like it doesn't even belong in the same atmosphere that I do. The rivers are bluer than blue, and the trees greener than green. Every tree here might as well be a redwood with the heights they all seem to reach.

"Glance," Phorbas says to me, "do not stare. The longer you look, the more familiar it becomes. When it becomes familiar, you forget how beautiful it once was."

He ruins my quiet moment of awe and inspiration. I share one look with Geiger and can tell from her wagging tail and pricked-up ears that we are committed, fully committed, to this mission now.

11

Chapter 11

Geiger blabbed the whole hike down. She must be so excited to make new friends with whom she cannot even speak. Now that we are closing in on the front gate of this cryptid city, though, she's gone a little quieter.

I think she has remembered that we are outsiders here and quite possibly the enemy of everyone around us. The caution she had of a solitary tree a few hours ago is now multiplying in her mind as we approach an entire town of potentially dangerous monsters. What are the laws of this place? Is it like the Westerns she loves to watch where the sheriff allows gentlemanly duels at high noon? Or is it lawless, every beast for themselves?

"I do not believe we brought enough bolas," she whispers, walking closer to my heels than ever before. "I also do not believe we will be welcome here. The command for operation '*RUN LIKE HELL*' is on standby."

"I do not need to understand her to know she is afraid," Phorbas says. "Tell your companion she may rest her amygdala. All of the boisterous beasts have surely found slumber by this

CHAPTER 11

hour."

His acknowledging that there are potentially dangerous creatures in these walls, albeit sleeping, probably, does not offer much comfort. The fact that the real baddies are nocturnal, just like me, offers even less comfort. When I rise at 8 PM, hoping for fried chicken and sourdough waffles, they will rise and hope to take a bite out of me. The first time we stop to rest, I might tinker with those bolas and see if I can make them a little more hair trigger.

We now stand at the town gate. An odd-shaped piece of plywood is nailed to the side, and the words "Welcome to Kelly" are crudely painted on. The wall is made of scraps of wood and metal. Some metal fencing here, some wooden boards there, and stacks of old tires everywhere. Where are they getting these materials? The front wall appears to wrap to two sides but slowly gets smaller and smaller as this town butts up to dense woods.

Before we enter through the shack-style walls, a slow and melancholic voice calls down from a watchtower above. "Phorbas, is that you?"

I look up and see one eye staring down at me. This creature's face appears to be nothing more than the one eye surrounded by shaggy fur. The creature is not standing; it is dangling. Its front and back claws are wrapped around a wooden beam overhead. With the long nails and its slow cadence coupled with the ever-watching Cyclops eye, I'd say this city guard is *Esuriens monstrum* — mapinguari — or starving monster.

Mapinguari are curious creatures. They are labeled as starving, not because their face is missing a mouth, but rather because their torso acts as one giant mouth. The creature slowly unfolds itself and peels away from its hanging spot. Landing on its feet, we see the starving monster in all its unsettling glory.

The cracked lips of its mouth stretch corner to corner from one side of its belly to the other. A monstrous tongue extends out to moisten its palate. The mouth hangs open, exposing two rows of carnivorous teeth. The starving beast is intimidating, but outrunning its pursuit shouldn't be a problem as it is considered a cousin of the sloth.

"Yes, Reggie, top of the morning to you," Phorbas answers. "My compatriots and I are just headed to the—"

"One dog and one extraterrestrial?" Reggie interrupts Phorbas.

"Hey, who you callin' extraterrestrial, buddy?!" I know my suit looks alien, but seriously?

Phorbas' wings spasm, almost like a hummingbird's. He turns his head to me without moving his shoulders. The dude is deeply unsettling sometimes.

"Forgive my foreign friend," Phorbas calls up to Reggie with his eyes still trained on me. "He is not quite used to our customs, you see. Nor is he used to thinking before speaking."

My temper usually burns hotter than a forgotten curling iron, but 'alien' is far from the worst thing I've been called. I'll let Phorbas handle the talking, seeing as his ugly mug is so charismatic.

Reggie literally lets out a belly laugh. "He will feel right at home then. Go on in."

He waves at Geiger as we walk through the town's portal. She may not understand his words, but she rises to her back feet and returns the wave in kind.

"The creatures are so funny here. I will make many new friends," she says after meeting exactly one creature.

The town is of rust and dust. Every step leaves a cloud of grit in its wake. Compared to the forest, the town of Kelly is a dusty metropolis. Within the first few feet, I spy gnomes, Loveland frogs, and yuccas. There are so many subspecies of sasquatch that the small identifiers can be hard to notice at a glance, like the difference between crocodiles and alligators or turtles and tortoises. Yucca, yowwie, yeti, they're all the same, sorta. A yucca, to take an example, has less hair than your standard 'squatch. Though this yucca appears to be stepping out of a barber shop, it could be a yowie wanting to feel a cooler autumn breeze.

The gnomes are scarfing down treats procured from a mini-washitu chef. The chef's shaggy beard, combined with his white headband and apron, do well to accompany his sign that peddles 'plant-based goods.' Two of the gnomes pass a treat behind their backs to fool a third gnome into believing it has vanished from reality. The stories I have heard of gnomes must hold water better than mop buckets. They snicker and jab like tiny grandparents with slapstick touches of humor.

Next to a pawn shop, a line has formed out the front of a nail salon. Who knew hygiene would be so important to these beasts? A jackalope waits to have her antlers filed, a megasloth waits to have his curling nails trimmed, and a giant beaver wishes to inquire about dental work. They all require different services of various body parts, but their eyes, whether it be two or one per skull, are all focused on us. An android, an above-water scuba diver, and a moth detective. Remaining low-key or simply blending in would be harder than mummy nuts.

The socializing of each community member hushes to a whisper when they take notice of our presence. Whether it's being a hider or being a human they don't like, I'm not sure. Regardless, I glaringly fit into both boxes squarely.

Fence gates operate as doors, and tent poles as cornerstones. Mild winds creak the entire town of rust. Everything is borrowed here. Nothing is new. Goblins must supply the economy with their proclivity for thievery.

I do wonder where all of this comes from. Surely, an insignificant goblin did not pack the five-pound wok from miles beyond the Spikes as a gift for the vegan chef. The sheer amount of hand-me-downs would take years of scavenging for a town this size. Either they have saddled sandworms, or there is a mode of transport that I have not been made aware of.

Phorbas guides us into what looks like a scrapyard in a town made of scrap. Walls of trash and tarnished metal stand taller than both of us. This trash heap takes up half the real estate of this town. One pile is all rust: bicycles, chain fence, busted home appliances. Another pile, all rubber, ranging from tractor tires down to training wheels. There are two shacks sitting side by side. Phorbas approaches one, hits the kick plate at the bottom of the door, and knocks it loose along with a puff of dirt.

"Forgive the mess, but genius is rarely tidy. Please, make yourselves at home for the day. You may rest here till dusk," Phorbas says without offering a grand tour of the single dirt-floored room.

I make fun of his house as if I own a mansion. But he assures me that this is not where he lives, just a place that he 'temporarily occupies for a small fee or favor.' He says this place is what it looks like. He acknowledges how weird it is for items on our side of the wall, miles away at this point, to be so common here that a landfill is needed. But, as usual, he promises to explain later. For now, I really need some rest.

Geiger and I have had our nerves cooked over this last half a day. A part of me feels excitement, maybe even a little wonder.

CHAPTER 11

But at the same time, I haven't had time to process any of this controlled chaos. Cryptids are living in an organized, functioning town. The thought breaks everything I've been taught. They *are* animals, but they're not *just* animals. Some have the same understanding as humans, and some are more simple-minded. It's not that humans can't also be considered simple, but our intelligence is still higher than that of other mammals. It's almost like the comparison cannot even be made.

I can't compare cryptids to humans because they are an array of different species. Some legends, like Yatee, can't even be classified because he was like something never seen before, something that has no equal on our side of the Spikes. I might as well be comparing insects to humans. I should have brought a sleep aid. My brain won't let me close my eyes. Is it weird to ask Phorbas for a dusting of that sleep powder?

12

Chapter 12

A hole in the patchwork roof allows a spotlight of sun to brighten my eyelids. I barely slept a wink's worth last night. Without sleep, our brains can't sponge out yesterday's dirty dishwater to allow a new clean stew for the next day to muck up. In half a night's sleep, my brain is half itself also, floating in the mire of yesterday.

There's no breakfast cooking, so the moth has at least a stitch of rudeness. Not that I could smell it through this rubber suit and helmet anyway. Wait, I'm not wearing my helmet. Where the hell is it?! My elbows hoist me up on my pillow in a flash.

It couldn't have gotten far. Maybe it shook loose in the night and rolled under the cot. Or caught between the cot and the wall. I frantically throw back my covers, knowing full well a helmet can't mask its shape under a thin sheet. Checking the floor next to me, I see it. Sitting right side up and facing toward me, the helmet's glass reflects a little sun back at me.

I scurry, dragging the bed sheets into the dirt with me. The helmet seals back onto my suit, accompanied by a large gulp of air racing its way to my lungs. But I wasn't drowning or floating

CHAPTER 12

in the vacuum of stars. Why did I start to hold my breath as if the air was the sought-after prize? A relief to be wearing it now. A horror to think of how long I was exposed.

No bacon frying, but neither is my skin as I check myself in a cracked window's reflection. Maybe it wasn't long. Or maybe the rads aren't applying constant pressure to me. The roof has some metal bits, maybe lead. There's a greater than zero chance I was slightly insulated. I'm looking for any way to gaslight myself into believing that I won't feel radiation sickness twist my stomach within the day's time.

Geiger is curled at the foot of my cot. How she didn't wake up in all that fuss, I will not question. I'm just glad I have a moment of peace without her high energy. When she wakes up, it'll be like a new parent at three in the morning bemoaning their next walk to check on the crying crib dweller. It's a pain to be tired, but it's agony to be tired and surrounded by the well-rested. I'll let her sleep as long as she would like.

My train of thought, or more like a train of confusion with no conductor controlling the furnace, is interrupted by singing. The smoothest voice, like one of those ladies in a red dress at a smoke lounge, is pulling me in like an *aqua mulier* or siren. A siren's song can't work on my now lead-shielded ears, so I look through the cracked glass again before deciding to venture out and follow the tune.

The closer I get, the better I can make out the melody. The words are right at the tip of my tongue; if the chorus comes back around, I might get on track with the faceless singer. I swing around a wall of rubber tires to see a small garden and a creature tending to it. The plants are not typical; they are familiar in shape but overgrown. Finally, I recognized her words.

I come to the garden alone. While the dew is still on the roses.

She is singing an old church hymn. My dad loved that one. *And the voice I hear, falling on my ear—*

"Hey, lady, some of us are trying to sleep," I bark at her.

She jumps, her hand covering her gasp. "Jesus! You nearly made me meet him!"

Her sense of humor is like an instinct. Her southern accent reminds me even more of the hymn's home.

I almost reply, "The look on your face made it worth it." But the look on her face is uncanny. She has human features and looks to be middle-aged, but there's more than that. For every human characteristic, she has an animalistic one. Brown iris and black pupils, but wrinkles around a snout nose. Gray hair in pigtail braids, but between pointed ears. What is she?

"Oh my Lord, you look just like your momma," she says in a cackle of disbelief.

Does this thing know my mom? Where the hell is that bug when you need him?

"Dr. Grace Carpenter and her brave little boy, Eric. But you ain't so little anymore, are ya?" she giggles.

I hate meeting old friends of my parents. 'I held you when you were just this big,' yeah, well, it must've been pretty noteworthy, seeing as I have zero memory of you or that event.

"How do you know my Mom?" I ask her. "Was she involved in a triage of yours or somethin'?"

The creature scrunches one corner of her mouth. "Goodness, that beast blood must've taken a better hold than I thought. No, she did not *triage* me. I was her colleague. If anything, we was *triaging* together," she answers with a tinge of offense.

"Beast blood?" I cautiously ask.

"You still don't know?" she makes a tutting noise as she returns to watering her plants. "They don't call 'em *hiders* for nothing, I reckon. Ain't it about time they let you in on a few secrets?" I catch her glance through the plant leaves. She is studying me up and down.

"I'm just a seeker. They don't keep me in the loop of a lot of the engineering stuff."

"Oh, that sciencey crap, " she says, "never liked it myself."

She begins telling me about the olden days when the labs had nothing but tables and filing cabinets. When the first computers were introduced to the place, she hated it. She and Mom grew close because my mom knew what she was doing with the machines. This lady needed Mom's help nearly every day, to the point where they just started sharing a workstation so Mom wouldn't have to keep interrupting her own work to be summoned elsewhere as tech support.

"When did you leave?" I interrupt her daydreaming of simpler times.

She takes a long pause to formulate her answer. "I left several years ago. Not long after your father..." she trails off.

I ask her another question quickly, not wanting her to drag me into that pity party. "What did you say your name was?"

"I'm Elenora, Elenora Fowler. You can call me Dr. Fowler if you'd like, but it's been a long time since I've heard that name. Most everyone I know just calls me Ellie." She takes a break from watering and extends her hand to me.

Her fingers are longer than a human's should be. And her nails are more like talons. Something changed this woman, but what? She still acts human, like a normal lady in a Halloween costume. I'm slow to accept the extended hand, but I shake it regardless. While I have her eye contact, a question slips out. It comes out like a mistake and without a prompt.

"What happened to you?"

Her smile fades. Her hand retracts to rest on her hip. With the other, she motions an invitation. We start walking through the maze of rubbish until we break back out into the town. She begins pointing out creatures and shacks, listing names of those who live where and who is in charge of what.

If this place had a mayor or any governing official at all, it would be Ellie. It's clear that she is home here. She says she only ever leaves the junkyard to eat or to deliver vegetables to the miniwashitu chef. She knows all the nooks and crannies, the secret gaps in the wall to get outside without going through the front gate. She is proud of this place.

"How do you exist here?" I ask. "Can you speak to them? Like I can?"

"Like you can?" she cuts her large eyes at me.

"Yeah, Phorbas didn't tell you?"

The look on her face is my answer. "Phorbas? Is that the moth you rolled in with? He ain't a stranger, that's for sure. But no, I can't talk to him or any of the others."

"He keeps talking about a friend he's got here," I say. "I just assumed it was you. We did stay in a shack in your yard last night, after all."

"Huh, you can really talk to him? Now that is somethin'." She pauses. "This town was here when I showed up. I didn't found the place or nothin'. The first couple of days were a little testy. It was easy to see that I made the folks here uncomfortable. I think they understood that I did and did not belong at the same time. I started staying in the yard with all the junk, and no one bothered me there. As more stuff came in, I started venturing out into the town. Taking spatulas to the cook, scissors to the barber, and broken binoculars to the guard. Couldn't say a word, but actions speak louder, they always say. Even made a nice little sign to put out front. Every town needs a name. Thought Kelly, like the green color, was a fine one."

"So the bug, you don't know him?" I ask.

"Acquaintances, maybe. He comes to town often. But I get the feelin' he don't like me. Always stuffs his hands in his pockets and heads the other way when I'm coming."

"He's never, like, said something without saying anything? You've never heard him in your head or nothin'?"

Ellie turns her chin to the side like a curious dog. "Telepathy, you mean? No. No, I guess not. That is interestin', though. Very interestin'."

"You can't speak to them," I begin. "You don't make money from them. Why the hell are you here?"

Our walk stops. She reaches down and rolls away a galvanized lid. A hole, a tunnel, is in a wall of junk toward the end of town and the outside of the junkyard. "Hyde's been hidin' too much from you," she says. "It's time they finally let you grow up a little. Wanna see somethin' cool?"

Here I was, thinking this was just a Sunday stroll. Maybe I should've woken Geiger for this.

The hole is so small we have to crawl through it. I shuffle my hands and knees through the dirt, careful not to snag my suit on any loose rust. We come out on the other side to an opening in the garbage, like a colosseum of hand-me-downs built around a gladiatorial pit. In the center of the pit is a metal platform. The metal isn't rusty; it's pristine and stainless. A half-circle arch sticks up from the flat platform, like a cave mouth that leads to nowhere.

Ellie holds out her palms toward the device, I guess you call it. "Waddya think?" she asks.

I think she built a stage. She did have a nice voice. Maybe she's gonna do concerts or something back here for the monsters.

"Okay, you got me," I say in defeat. "What am I looking at here?"

"You ever wished you could just get somewhere real fast? Be there in a flash?" she asks.

"Like to the point? I'd love to get there fast."

"Oh, oh, one," she says, rolling her eyes. "Jiminy. This device lets us do that. We call it a *teleporter*. *Tele*, like the vision. *Porter*, like the mailman."

I take a loop around this invention and try not to laugh at her. She is sweet, but there's no way the rads haven't fried her one crayon short of a full set if she thinks this thing can magically make things appear.

"Tele. Porter." I say. "You're joking, right? Is it some kind of trick or somethin'? Stage magic?"

"There is a stage, and it certainly feels like magic. But this is real."

"You've been reading too many penny dreadfuls, lady," I reply. "Sure looks techy. Thought you hated that kinda thing."

Ellie hikes one foot onto the platform and lifts herself onto it. "They put me through a whole lot of training to properly handle all its moving parts," she says. "It ain't been up and running very long. Well, ain't been up and running *correctly* very long."

She has said *we* twice now. "Who is 'we'?" I ask.

"We. Us. Hiders. You and me. Come on now, thought you was smarter than this, oh, oh, one."

"What are you saying? 'Oh, oh, one'? What is that?"

She snickers with a grin I haven't noticed till now. It's wide. Wider than a human jaw should allow. "Oh, oh, one. Zero, zero, one. That's you, sweetheart." Circling the stage with a hand on the arch, her nails scrape against the metal.

CHAPTER 12

"Me? 001? They stopped using that badge system when they switched the doors to retina scans," I reply.

"They really have kept so much from you," she says. "How can you speak to everything under the sun and not know a lick about nothin'?" Shrill and piercing, she cackles out a laugh.

A small dose of adrenaline begins to seep its way into the rhythm of my heartbeat. Is it because of her or just an anxious fear of what she will say next?

Before I can speak, she continues toward me. "This teleporter does work. And here, before too long, I'll show ya."

"Where does it go?" the question escapes me.

"It goes back to where you came from. Where I'll return you to. You ain't supposed to be here."

Her back raises like a cat readying its defense. Something about her eyes is changing. Every time they meet mine, they look less and less like Ellie and more and more like nobody at all.

"Ellie, why would you send me back? I just got here. Phorbas wants my help. He says the cryptids need me, need us."

A voice comes out of her body, but it's not the southern honey I'm used to hearing from her. It's deeper. It matches the black fog that is setting into her irises. "What do you think comes and goes through this gate, 001? The cryptids don't need your help. They need you to get your nose out of where it doesn't belong."

That name again, 001. Ellie, or whatever the creature in front of me is, she plans to attack me. I can feel it. My instinct of survival. The battle in my mind is whether I use that adrenaline to run and get away from her or not move an inch. Stand here and fight.

"What's that name you keep calling me?" I ask.

She tuts me silent, "You don't need that silly helmet. You slept fine all day. Take it off, and let me see you face to face."

"You're losing it, Dr. Fowler."

"Didn't sleep so well? Aww, is little Eric still having the nightmares?" Her voice is no longer her own. It's contorting itself with every syllable.

"What — what did you just say?"

"Experiment 001, Eric Carpenter," her gravel voice begins. "Subject has recovered from all sustained wounds in 72 hours since insertion. Wounds include a skull fracture, compound tibia fracture, dislocated wrist, cuts, and bruises sustained to the arms, legs, abdomen, and head. The subject is displaying nightly cold sweats and extreme anxiety—"

"Enough! What the hell are you going on about?!" I explode. What game is she playing?

"They let the first experiment rest in the comfort of their insulated home. But they throw the second out with the trash," she says. Her visible frustration is mounting. "We are the first of our kind. We shouldn't be enemies."

"Whatever you're meaning, whatever you're thinking, let's talk about this. We don't have to be enemies." I don't understand her. Her mind is racing, and mine can't keep up. I am saying anything to try and back her down from what is feeling inevitable.

Her spine is hunched. She is pacing her way toward me with her knees facing out. Her expression shifts from the Ellie I thought I knew to the scowl of a de-feathered bird.

"What did you let them do to you?"

"You're not the only one who had no choice!" she retorts in anger. A sliver of her soft southern charm returns. "Dr. Hyde's been real sick. He said what we were doin' would help him. Help us all. He wants a cure for his death, but not just that. He wants to take a lap around other humans. He wants strength, he wants intellect, he wants to be ancient of days."

A cure-all. He thinks the beasts hold the cure to life. It's a pretty sound theory, considering they have adapted to unlivable conditions in the rads. But still, the lifespan of these beasts varies from species to species. Every biological clock ticks down. The cells can only copy so many times before the copy of the copy of the copy starts to show its flaws. He's gone as far as genetic splicing? Is that what's wrong with her? Her very DNA makeup must be modified, and it's taking over.

"He's on a fool's errand then," I interject. "Cryptids die just like we do. Miraculous as they are, they're still just beasts, animals, flesh, like you and me."

"You feel it. You're home here, too. You feel alive here." She takes a step toward me and points to my ankle. "That hole in the suit, that's enough, and you know it is. Radiation is like water. One small opening lets the whole wave in."

Ya Te Veo had opened my suit with his thorns. A small gash. Being swept up in my gratitude for being alive, I didn't even give any thought to it. Ellie is right; radiation doesn't need an invitation. If the door is cracked, it comes in and sits a spell.

"You don't know what you're talking about," I bark. "I haven't felt any different. I've got no burns."

"Open your eyes and see," she says. "Why don't you burn? Why can you speak? Why are your fists clenchin'?"

I repeat my question with solemn resolve, "What did they do to you?"

She is staring a hole in the platform below her. "Trial—genome—ahool," she stutters words in a barely formed structure as the beast within her fights again for control.

"We always have a choice, Dr. Fowler. Please, consider your next one wisely."

She pauses like she's been frozen in time. Her head jerks straight up to the sky. Her neck wretches and bones crack to the tune of her spinal column raising itself a few notches of vertebrae. She is still as stone.

Her jaw hangs open as she answers me in a shaky voice that is all human and no beast. As a teardrop paints its way to the corner of her mouth, she says, "First was a little boy and his frantic mother. All of creation began with Adam, so it shall be for us. But do not fear. Eve killed her Adam, too."

She throws her head down as it snaps into place on her jagged, craned spine. All semblance of Ellie is gone. What remains is a beast scorching the air with its piercing shriek. A shriek I have heard only once before: the church. Thin skin, like bat wings, hangs down from her arms.

Whatever she needed, whatever she was facing, Dr. Hyde took advantage of her weakness for his own benefit. I am so sorry, Dr. Fowler. You did not deserve this. Forgive me for the dirt I'm about to rub your ugly snout in.

13

Chapter 13

Before I can make another appeal to Ellie, she is pouncing on me. Her gangly fingers and lanky arms make it hard to escape her wingspan. I backpedal away from each swipe and lunge of her claws. Eventually, I will run out of room in this junk arena; I need a plan.

I take my eyes off her for an instant to better assess my surroundings. In a flash, she closes the distance. She is not letting me get a chance to think. I deter her advancement once more but feel my heel hit against the wall. There's no more running away.

Conceding the fact that I will not escape this fight unscathed, I completely turn my back on her like a moron. The one thing you should never do when facing a wild animal, but what choice did I have? My eye spots an old pipe among the trashed treasures. Its base is fitted with a tee joint, which is perfect for helping me maintain a usable grip on the makeshift weapon.

I reach out to the junk pile to free my Excalibur. Ellie buries her claws in my back as I do. My outstretched arm recoils as I can feel her phalanges dig into my lats. My elbow reflexively spins me around to ward her off as her claws dig a burrow down my back strap of muscle. I can't see it, but I can feel it. She opened a gaping wound.

My healing acts almost immediately on any bump, scrape, or bruise. One thing I have learned about accelerated healing, though, is that it comes at its own cost. The deeper the wound, the heavier the blood flows out of my skin; the hotter the burning sensation of rapid healing is. The pain of the injury is there, but it is not alone. Every ailment is accompanied by a burn that I can only equate to peroxide entering a forgotten paper cut. But twice the pain is worth the trade-off for the ten times restoration. The pain, the torn flap in my rad suit, she did some damage but also managed to mightily piss me off.

The burst of my reflexive action flings Ellie into the stack of trash. This buys me enough time to shake free the metal pipe, my only defense. I grab the stop-gap weapon by its hilt and take an unsure stance. I've not exactly been trained in hand-to-hand combat. Seekers learn a few moves that help with leveraging against large assailants, but I was never prepared for fighting a human hybrid with old plumber equipment. Ellie bounces up to her feet and gnashes her teeth at me. I'm not the only one getting angry.

She leaps into the air. Her feet are at eye level with me for a moment before her weight comes crashing onto me. She snaps her bite at me over and over. Her jagged teeth snap closed on the shield of my helmet. The glass webs my vision, masking her assault behind the safety of my blindness.

Taking one end of the pipe in each hand, I force its way under the bite of her jaw. She crunches down onto the metal. Like a horse with no reins, I struggle to hold on. Her strength is incredible. It is far beyond what can be expected of a woman in terms of her size and age. The height she was able to achieve on her pounce was higher than what should be humanly possible. This mutagen, the change in her DNA, has affected more than just her stature but her power as well.

Ellie grits down on the bar between her jaws and flings it free from my hands. With a swift flick of her head, she discards the piece of metal and brings a bite down into my shoulder.

I scream in anguish. Feeling the serrated edge of teeth carve away at my flesh churns my stomach. In the pain and in the anger, I feel rationale leaving my mind. Thoughts creep into the backdoor of my subconscious. Voices telling me that this really could be my end.

In my bubble of convenience back at the Hyde Foundation, survival is not a concern. Every meal is provided, and the roof over my head is paid for by someone else. My shield of comfort is webbing worse than the glass shielding my face. Never have I feared, truly feared, losing my life until this very moment.

My vision blurs into a red haze. With every growl of the beast on top of me, I can hear my heartbeat rising and falling, not knowing which way to go, not knowing if the fight is beginning or if it is already lost.

Whispers of memories come to the forefront of my mind. A time of peace, when my world was the safest it had ever been. I'm in the woods with my dad.

"Why do these trees grow so tall?" I ask him.

"They're called redwoods," he says. "They're the biggest trees in the world. Not just any tree can reach that size."

"Do the other trees feel bad for not being so big?"

He laughs, "I'm not sure they worry about that. Every tree is doing its best, and most times, that's enough."

"I heard somebody call you a redwood. Does that make me

one, too?"

Dad looks down at me and then kneels to my level. "Even a tiny seed can grow into something mighty. It just has to refuse to stay buried. Don't let anyone or anything keep your face in the dirt. Always fight back and stand back up, nice and tall. That's what makes you a redwood."

My thoughts return to the problem at hand. My fingers dig into the soil around me. My body is fighting to regain strength. I feel myself stretching my own limits, stretching for something I have never needed before. My body is deciding which way it ought to respond — fight or flight. But my brain is telling it, *I ain't running anywhere.*

Ellie rares back from her bite to relish in her success, my blood flowing down her grin. While she celebrates prematurely, I hurl my fist at her jaw with strength that doesn't feel like I own it. My punch connects squarely and sends her careening off of her perch. She skates across the dirt on all fours, leaving cornrows where her fingers dug for traction.

My vision is red — literally. I am seeing her through a new lens. The confident and relentless beast from a moment ago now has a look of contemplation on her face. Whatever is happening to me now, she feels it, too.

A scream erupts from me when I stand. The burning of my skin knitting itself together has never felt so agonizing. If this pain is anything close to what I felt that day at the church, no wonder my mind chose to forget it all. Blood flowing down my back feels like it is releasing tears of its own. My shoulder is drooped down. Her barrage of bites must have severed tendons, leaving it limp. With the one arm I can actually raise above my neck, I remove my helmet and slide the top part of this jumpsuit off of my shoulders.

CHAPTER 13

Half-naked and half-strength is not an ideal situation to win a fight, but at least it can now be considered one. Not wanting to lose my momentary advantage, I charge at Ellie. I send another fist headed toward her temple, but she slides out of the way. Her body slinks down, crinkled together like a snake waiting for the right time to strike. I shuttle my knee at her in an instant. My body is moving faster than either of us anticipated, and my knee connects. I can nearly feel her orbital bones concave around the shape of my leg. The hit was more than effective.

Ellie stumbles away off balance. She has now suffered as many critical blows as I have. As far as I'm concerned, we are even. I do not advance towards her. I want to see how she retaliates, if at all. I know she is more than this monster that is taking hold of her, and I want to see if some sense has been knocked into her and if the true Dr. Fowler can return to the surface. The stars and ducklings spinning around her head must not have lasted long because she recoils back into her stance. She begins a run at me, and I do the same toward her. She is nimble, but I am confident that I have a strength advantage. If we collide, I win.

My feet dig into the earth like baseball cleats. My mind is racing, telling me to charge, attack, take down. Ellie has no quiver in her resolve. She is digging her claws in the ground ahead of her stride. Ellie makes her leap into the air. I was hoping to be close enough to tackle her out, but she did not jump at me like I was anticipating.

Ellie lurches to the side and clings to the junk wall. She springboards off and launches over my head. I feel one hand grab my shoulder and the other eviscerate down into the flesh of my back. Her momentum drags me down. We crash to the ground. I am on top of her, but she has my back. I cannot swing my weight enough to roll over with only one arm at my disposal. She bites down into me again, and a roar bursts from my soul.

My head is thrashing. Anything I can do to put up a struggle. My hands are unable to reach her. Her jaw is gnawing its way deeper into my back. I feel helpless again. My thrashing becomes more and more alert to my present situation. I squirm to try and hoist any angle and roll any weight, but I am failing. Another scream escapes me, but it is not the scream of a man in pain, it is like the wailing of a trapped animal.

My howls echo off the walls around us and shake enough things free from their rest that dust begins to fill the air. Slinging my neck forward and backward, trying to make contact with her horrid face, I see the dust whip up and down with my hair. The red and brown hues of dry clay mud look all the same color through my red eyes. But one color is not like the rest.

I see vivid swirls of purple dance in the clouds of this junkyard dirt. This purple is unmistakable by the way it glimmers in the light, a questionable last hope. I continue knocking my head around like I'm grasping at motivation for another lap around the track. The sharp grip of Ellie's bite begins to relax. Even without seeing her, I can feel the fading strength. Seconds pass, and her arms fall to the side. I roll off of her weak body and onto my knees. She is completely out cold. Her body's transformation is undoing itself. Her features are becoming more human, or at least as human as they get.

My lame arm is resting on top of my leg. The sea of pooling blood around me forms clumps of dirt islands. My head drops after a full sigh expels from my lungs. A few purple sparkles fall from my forehead, and I watch them sweep away in the wind. My eyes are wide open, but I have no expression. The only thing I feel at this moment is the adrenaline of victory being quickly replaced by the shame of realization, the shame of knowing what I am. An experiment. A monster. A moth.

14

Chapter 14

My bum arm is resting on my good arm that's folded across my stomach. The trail of blood behind me has slowed to a trickle. My feet barely lift off the dirt as I shuffle along, not knowing where I'm even headed. For now, straight into the woods, as far as my strength will carry me. If I walk into another carnivorous shade tree, so be it. If I walk to the edge of a cliff, I'll take one big step off. If I walk to a plunge pool, I'll jump in and pretend it's a drawn bath.

So much frustration and confusion is steaming inside me, but the shock makes it all feel hollow. I feel, and surely look, like a zombie from an old horror flick. Dad always liked old awful movies. You knew Dad was stressed out if you heard popcorn popping, grainy dialogue, and the recliner folding out. He could always escape for a little while into movies.

My escapism was always a little more literal. Anytime I got upset or frustrated, I just wanted to go — do something to get away from whatever the source was. Dad would help me strap into my light-up sneakers, and we would just go. We were headed nowhere, in particular. We'd walk until something

CHAPTER 14

distracted me, or I got tired enough to lose the energy that worrying requires. I was hoping the old walking away method would work for me right now. As my mom would say, "Hope in one hand and shit in the other — when you wash one, you rub the two all over it."

I fled from Ellie as soon as I could gather the will to get on my feet again. Not knowing how she'd wake up, I didn't want to have to survive another round. Also, a thought crept in that maybe this is what Phorbas had planned all along. Maybe Ellie sent him to find me and bring me to her so she could do away with me herself. She loved blabbing all that vendetta-sounding stuff about how I was '001' and how 'Eve killed her Adam.' Which isn't even a hundred percent true; Adam ate the fruit knowing the consequences as well. He knew better or should've known better. Maybe that part applies to me. Should I have known better?

Ellie seemed nice enough, but something took hold of her. Can she control it, or was that an accident? Not to mention, I'm the only one who knows the moth. They both could be lying to me. Did he know she would freak out and eat my trapezius for lunch? Occam's Razor would have me believe the simplest explanation is the truth, but I currently don't know what that might be.

My eyes, matching the moth's red hashed look, are spacing out. The forest floor beneath me might as well be a thousand feet below. My brain has a way of flooding itself with too many thoughts for me to keep track of. In those times, I enter what I call *autopilot*.

Some entire days, I've lived on autopilot. Some sleepless nights I lie awake in this factory default mode. I'm still me, and I'm still here, but I'm a shell. I ignore my own cares and just let my body move itself. The simplest thoughts are the ones I deal with. The more complex ones sink down deep somewhere into the subconscious. That song Ellie was singing. Where did she leave off?

And He walks with me
And He talks with me
And He tells me I am his own

A twig snaps behind me and interrupts my singing. Fashionably late, as usual, I hear footsteps falling in behind me. Without looking back, I holler, "I'm really not in the mood to talk right now. Maybe later, after my eyes stop looking like kaleidoscopes."

No response is called back to me. No attitude, no one-liner, must be someone I don't know then. Wondering what fresh hell could be stalking me so close, I whip my head around. To my surprise, I see no one. Not to my surprise, my neck spikes in pain — no more whipping, gotcha.

"Hello," I call out again. I wait for a good dramatic beat and turn to continue my walk. The sound of steps is still there but faint. Their gait is so similar to mine that I can only hear their footfalls when my weakened cadence is not being matched exactly. What a smart stalker.

"If you plan to attack my back, I'm afraid someone has beat you to it," I poke, again trying to coax a response.

"You can't outrun it," I hear a whisper say.

The reply makes me jump. Whoever that was sounded like their lips were pressed against my ear — or both ears. The ghostly voice felt all around me. But again, I see no one.

"It's a good thing I'm not running then. I'm just walking." Being a smartass is my most trusted defense mechanism.

A sinister laugh echoes off the bark around me, but that is all

CHAPTER 14

they give. Not feeling particularly threatened, albeit creeped out, I place one foot in front of the other and keep going. I've got too much on my mind to worry about this — whatever it is.

"For my peace of mind, what are you?" I ask.

"Peace of mind is not here. We feel greatly burdened, don't we?" it whispers back.

Looking like a corpse left out in the rain, I am not impressed with his assessment. "HA, what gave it away?" I shout, to no reply.

An awful thought bubbles to the top of my self-wallowing soup. I left Geiger, didn't tell her where I was going, or that I was mugged by a she-devil; nothing. She might still be resting, not even missing me. She makes friends so quickly and has such a social personality that she might not care that I'm gone at all. Maybe she will at first, but once she latches on to someone new, I'll be forgotten all the same. I was never outgoing enough for her, and she will probably feel relief when I am gone. She might feel like she can finally do more of what she wants instead of having to protect me all the time. Mom has always done her best with me. Hell, she even built me an android partner just so I'd have someone who could stand to be around me.

Mom, oh no. What is she gonna think? Losing her husband and now her son? Or would losing me be more like losing your science project? Maybe all these years, that's what she's done. Kept me in the Hyde Foundation so I'd be within reach in case I morphed into a monster like Ellie. How could I be such an idiot? She made me live in that place because I was an experiment; I was company property. Letting me live a life on my own would have been a waste of their resources and profit margins. Letting myself fester and rot could be one last middle finger to that whole operation. I could disappear and make them start from

001 all over again. Let Mom attach that dog's leash to someone else. Let them get babysat their whole life.

"If those damn footsteps get any louder, I won't be able to hear myself think!" my thoughts explode. I spin around to try and confront the owner of said feet. In the corner of my eye, I see a man, a tall man, duck in behind a tree. His witch-like fingers nearly wrap around the entire trunk. He is wearing a stovepipe hat, and one eye is peering around the bark.

In a eureka moment, I yell to him, "I caught you! What now? Did I win your game of hide-and-seek?"

"You win my name if I get to know yours."

Under my breath, I scoff, "These beasts and their shit-ass names. I'm Eric."

"I am called Sam," the man replies.

"Well, what do you want, Sam?"

"Your broken spirit called me here. Walking to clear your mind has succeeded only in clouding it," he says, speaking as if he can see into my thoughts. "Keep walking."

His command to walk sends an echo from my mind down to my feet. It was his voice and something more, like something I felt instead of heard. Without hesitation, I walk.

"Where are we going?" I ask, my voice sounding stiff.

"To absolution," the spirit answers.

My body is healing, but I have not changed my pace or composition. There is something comforting about having my arm draped across my body like I can at least embrace myself. My mind is a rad storm, the thoughts growing increasingly toxic. Walking across the forest floor, I was cautious of my steps at first. But now my chin is buried in my sternum, and I could not care less about what I might wander into.

"Do you miss your father?" Sam asks.

CHAPTER 14

"Every day."

"Why haven't you joined him then?"

"He's somewhere I can't go yet," my voice cracks while trying to speak about him.

"I can show you the way," Sam's kind voice offers.

"If I had wings, I could fly there," a teardrop at the end of my nose shivers me.

"It only takes one leap of faith."

"One leap?" my voice stammers.

"The rush of wind will quiet your mind, give you peace. Just one leap, Eric." Sam's voice is in my ear like a consoling touch on my shoulder.

"No, I — I can't," I combat.

"Don't you want the pain to stop? The sleepless nights to end?"

"Eric?" I hear my name from a different voice in the distance. I do not investigate. I keep walking.

"He misses you too, *Eric,*" Sam says. "So incredibly much."

"*Eric,* stop!" the two voices overlap on my name, swirling around my head like pesky insects.

"One leap, Eric."

"Eric, no!"

The voices combat.

"You just need a little push."

"No, I — I don't want to," I object.

"Fly, Eric! One more step."

I plant my feet, and they don't move again. This spirit, Sam, is playing a mind game. Thoughts of inadequacy, questioning the motives of my friends, the distrust. All of it has to be his influence. What is this?

"My body is what's broken," I say, "not my mind."

"Do it. Do it now!" The once-calm spirit commands.

I am my father's son, the unmovable redwood. He thinks I'll check out this easy: let the Hyders win, let him win, just like that?

My thoughts are clear again, finally. My feet might as well be growing roots because I have control over them again, and they aren't taking another step. The spirit, in all his frustration, flies out from behind his hiding place.

Hiding no more, he appears in front of me. His stature is long and thin. On his face sit nothing but two eyes, no nose, and no mouth. He bends down close to see me eye-to-eye with his furrowed brow.

"So," I say, "the urban legends are true. A forest spirit that claims spirits for the forest. Why, though?"

Looking into his eyes, I see pain. A solemn solitude that feeds on the lost. Playing in my mind like a slideshow projection, I see the countless victims he has influenced and the endless depression he has fermented into despair. His brow is slowly loosening its coil.

"Stop," he whispers.

"Stop what?"

"How can you do this?" he whimpers.

The slideshow playing in my mind is from his memory. It has to be. How could I see these things if it were not him forcing me or allowing me? If he isn't the one making me watch it, then am I making him?

"Release me, end this now!" he barks at me, but he seemingly cannot break my stare.

Watching him writhe in horror gives a darker part of me a good smile. I have no idea what is going on or how I'm doing this, but I hope it never ends. Sam reaches his crooked fingers up to his face. If he cannot look away, then he must stop looking somehow. First, the nail of his pointer finger, then the tip of his thumb, squelch into his sockets. His scream covers the viscous sound of retinal fluid escaping in a pop. Rather than facing his past, the souls he has tormented, he has chosen to gouge his own eyes. Today, those souls receive justice, and Sam serves his penance.

The spirit's eyes ooze something like black milk. His form disperses into smoke. A hand weighing down my shoulder snaps me out of my trance as if Sam was only a dream.

"You should not be treading so closely to the edge," Phorbas imparts to me.

"What?" I shake my head and take a look around. I stand at the edge of a great waterfall. Only now can I hear the roar of the water as it rushes the rocks and cascades below.

"Could you not hear my calling over the crashing water? You looked like you were about to..." Phorbas trails off. He is staring at my eyes, my new eyes. He is probably also noticing how the dirt on my face is washed clean in tear-sized streaks. Does he know about Ellie yet? Would knowing about her assault on me unmask him as well?

"There was a voice, a spirit," I say. "He wouldn't let me think. He had control and was sending me spiraling down into—"

"You are bloodied, brother," Phorbas stops me. "You should rest." He takes off his dusty coat and throws it around my shoulders. He grabs my elbows and ushers me to a seat on the ground. "A run-in with Walking Sam, I know it well. Reserved for the lost who do not wish to be found. Let us sit a spell and enjoy the water. Two monsters are enough for one day."

15

Chapter 15

I must have dozed off. My body might have shut me down to allow the healing to use all my energy. I don't feel any burning, and all I hear is the loud rush of the waterfall. That is a peaceful sound. My mind is no longer revolting against itself, which is also a good sign. A nap surely does cure what ails. I'm not sure how much time has passed, but as soon as my eyes open, they close shut from the blinding green light on Geiger's flashlights.

"He's up! I knew you'd be okay. Phorbas wasn't so sure, I think, but I knew better. '*HARD TO KEEP CARPENTER MEN DOWN,*'" Geiger vibrantly voices, utilizing her own voice and a little help from Moms.

It's evening twilight. I slept for hours. My head is pulsing. It feels like that first hour after a crippling migraine where your skull feels like it's trying to breathe. Phorbas is packing a bundle of sticks with his sleeves rolled up as if he's been hard at work.

"Rise and shine, brother," Phorbas exhales as he plops the sticks to the ground. "We were not sure how long you'd be in your slumber, so we were preparing to build a fire."

CHAPTER 15

"Building a fire? We're campers now, huh?" I ask in a gravelly morning voice.

"We didn't lie to 'GARRETT' after all," Geiger points out. "We could not leave you out here on your own. Not in this cold. Temperatures are expected to drop to 50 degrees Fahrenheit tonight. Side effects of improperly regulated body temperature include hypothermia, irritability, loss of food satiation—"

"We simply would not leave you," Phorbas interrupts Geiger's rambling. "Plus, I had a fear that you would potentially enter a cocoon state, which requires a comfortable heat to offer any benefit."

I sigh at the sound of that. So now I could just 'enter a cocoon state' at random. With a new-found perspective on my life, I have so many moth-related questions. How does a caterpillar know it's a moth or a butterfly? Does it just hatch and hope for the best? Are gloomy larvae turned into butterflies for cosmic comedic irony?

Phorbas interrupts my thoughts as if he can see the spiral forming. "I do have the theory that your healing may be your body's own form of cocooning — not requiring entire silken insulation."

"What could possibly make you think either of those things?" I ask.

Phorbas picks his jacket off of me and points to my back. "Go to the water. See your reflection."

I walk to the flowing stream and try to find a spot calm enough that my reflection is visible. First, I examine my face and my identity. Am I still Eric on the outside, or was I forever changed? My eyes are not red, and they do not look like insect eyes. That is a relief. Maybe, like Ellie, some of my transformation is not permanent. However, some of her features have been permanently changed, and perhaps that's only a matter of time for me. For now, I am happy to see a familiar, albeit dirty and bloody, face looking back at me. The bite on my front side is healed, tender to the touch, but healed. I turn my back to the water to examine my wounds there. Phorbas' theory now makes a little more sense. The two clawings down each side of my spine have silken wrappings over them, almost like they've been bandaged with gauze.

"Well, that's new." I look to Geiger and Phorbas for affirmation, but there is none. The two of them stand with their arms folded. The looks on their faces are like mechanics examining the vast amount of work needing to be done to a piece of junk clunker. "Ever seen anything like this before, mothman?" I try to get one of them to speak, at least.

Phorbas shakes his head. "Cocoons, of course. Cocoon-like scabbing, certainly not."

Wanting to change the subject from my anomaly that is increasing my anxiety with every intrusive idea, I ask a question to hopefully lessen a different anxious school of thought. "I'm guessing you two know about Ellie?"

Geiger says she knew Dr. Fowler many years ago at the Hyde Foundation, but she had no idea this was what had become of her. Phorbas met Ellie many years ago when she displayed more human traits than beast ones. He said it didn't take long to deduce something was off about a human living freely in the rads, and eventually, he knew something about her was wrong. He insists that Ellie did not send him after me. She was part of what he wanted me to see, but mostly, he wanted me to see the secret work she was doing. He maintains that she was not at the root of my coming here.

"Kelly is a haven of information," Phorbas says. "Creatures

of all tribes and climates wind up here at some point. New perspectives and new ideas all combine in this town. Perhaps the hiders thought she would blend well here. Perhaps they thought no one would notice her. We are not dumb animals like they would have you believe. They sent a wolf in sheep's clothing, and all of the sheep knew."

"Do you think they wanted her to kill me?"

Phorbas replies, "Her mind, her body, is so closely knit together now with feral fight or flight instincts. Think of how her threatening presence transformed your own body. Hers responds in the same manner. In her mind, she knew your potential, so her body assessed you as a threat. Or, perhaps, she played us all the fool. The wolf lay low, very low, in the sheep pasture."

I scoff, "My potential? What does that even mean?"

Phorbas' finger rests on his chin in a thinking posture. "It is no secret that Ellie still works for the Hyde Foundation in some capacity," he says. "They often enter through her teleporter to deliver items and messages. Perhaps she has access to their tests. Perhaps she knows the tests performed on you."

"Dr. Fowler was unconscious last we saw her. She cannot be questioned on our suspicions at this time," Geiger adds, mimicking Phorbas' pose.

"You didn't know about the experiment on me? You didn't know I was a moth?" I ask both of them

Phorbas answers first. "I did not know of the DNA tampering, no. However, on our first meeting, I felt a familiarity. My intuition told me that you were a friend, a brother, but I did not fully understand it till now."

Geiger follows up. "I was never made aware of any human testing. Your mother always told me that you were special, and she was always right. But I did not know she meant it in this way. It was my understanding that you were just 'COOLBEANS.'"

Pretty sure she got that voice recording from a commercial on the radio about pintos you store in the freezer. Neither of them are liars. Any mistake or overlooking that led us all here, we've been pawns in someone else's game. The bliss of ignorance is not one we will experience for much longer. The... *people* in front of me are the only ones I can trust anymore. The three of us will face the remaining mysteries together.

Talking to my friends has made me realize how distant and untrustworthy I have treated them. Phorbas has defended me from sasquatches, Yat-te-veo, and now has revealed the true nature of who is actually working against me. Geiger's loyalty to me could never be fully detailed. But even still, I've been vile to both of them. When I am bleeding and unconscious, they build a fire to keep me warm because they'd rather rough it in the sticks than even try to move me and risk further injury. If I were them, I'd never stick around this selfish asshole, *Eric*. From here out, they are my only allies. Not Ellie, not even Mom. Not until we have a better understanding of what the hell is going on here.

"If hiders are using the teleporter to get cryptids out of the rads, I guess we are officially aligning as their enemies," I say and wait for head nods. "If I'm gonna be much of any help, can you familiarize me with some of my new *capabilities*?"

Phorbas grins that awful smile. "Two moths are better than one."

16

Chapter 16

Geiger is heading back to town to spy on Ellie. Keep your friends close and your enemies under a microscope. Before they came looking for me, they found Ellie out cold in the dirt. Phorbas carried her into the shed by the garden. While me and Phorbas go over a few moth ins and outs, Geiger will see if it's safe for me to return to town. Geiger nabbed me a change of clothes from somewhere, and I didn't want to ask where. Even if they are old and dingy, it's better than shredded and bloody. Besides, I think we have determined that the rad suit is no longer functional and no longer necessary.

Nightfall is upon us, but my eyes hardly notice. Phorbas thinks the ever-present dose of radiation is what's causing me to show signs of my moth DNA. He's probably right, but it does make me wonder how far these transformations will go.

"You are certain that the darkness does not hinder your sight?" Phorbas asks as we walk down to the bottom of the waterfall. "We bugs do not do well in water."

"That's a good place to start. What are a moth's strengths?" I ask. "The hiders know next to nothing about you guys."

Phorbas takes a few silent steps and then answers, "We hide in the dark well, we can fly, we are intelligent, and we have great lifespans." His answer trails a bit before he picks back up, "I suppose you do not have the necessary requirements to blend into a nightfall or to take flight."

"My intelligence is lacking, too," I interject. "And that lifespan is gonna be a lot shorter if I keep getting attacked by random crap," I joke, but it naturally leads into a lecture.

"You have an innate ability to find a skirmish, that is certain. But you also find ways to win those engagements. That is an intelligence every king who ever lived wished they had. The words we speak can either poison or strengthen those around us. Speak kinder to yourself, brother, and notice how the world around you follows suit," he drones on. "You have been blessed with speech understood by every ear that hears. Do not waste it by spewing venom."

He's taking this mentor thing too seriously, but I know he means well. In the process of turning a new leaf, I don't smart off at him. His advice is good, it's wise. Only fools despise correction, and I've been enough of a fool to last an entire lifetime. Maybe a small amount of correction is okay for today.

While we hike down to non-precariously perched land, I flurry Phorbas with questions. Are all moths this polite? Do you wear gym shorts on warm days? Can we go to a moth village? Are you married? Do moths get married? How does the suit fit over your wings? Can I get a suit? Will I feel the urge to chew holes in it? Most of my questions are dismissed with quips that I believe are jokes or at least half-jokes. But one question halts Phorbas.

"Why do moths fly at bug zappers?" I ask. "Can't they tell it's dangerous?"

CHAPTER 16

We are at the bottom of our hill descent. While he catches his breath a little, he takes a long look at me and answers, "Wander in the darkness long enough, and you will find any light worth dying for."

Phorbas asks how I was able to subdue Ellie. I tell him it was the same way he subdued the sasquatch, except it came from the purple hair on my head. He's quiet a moment, then asks about my strength. I tell him that it felt overwhelming, that my joints felt like they might explode from exerting the force of my strength. He asks if I feel that power now, but I do not. He seems to think that my abilities were brought on by my will to survive, my fight or flight. When my body decided to fight, it meant it. And now that I am back to 'normal,' my body is also back to 'normal.'

I ask about Ellie, though. She has traits of her own, such as her ahool DNA, written across her face. In theory, she has lived with her mutagen just as long as I have. So why, then, do I not show the same signs? We decided that her exposure, overexposure, to radiation vastly altered her. Whereas I stayed relatively rad-free until a day or so ago. Maybe if we wrap up all of our Spike business, I can get out of here before changes manifest a little more permanently.

My eyes don't look like moth eyes, but they are beginning to see like them. My body has never produced silk before, but my back is currently covered in it. My changes are accelerating fast. Big bug eyes are kinda cute on women, on Molly, but *these* bug eyes make a monster out of anyone.

"Strength, spore, silk, are there any other abilities you have displayed?" Phorbas alliterates at me.

I tell him about when he found me walking to the waterfall's edge, about the spirit that brought my suppressed thoughts to the forefront, the great feeling of dread I felt like I was going to drown in, and how the entity responsible appeared to me and looked into my eyes. When he did, all he saw was his pain, his past, and his dread, and he drowned in it.

"Stare," Phorbas says, almost like a question. "A legend among legends. If what you say is true, you are the only moth I know who possesses such an ability. They made you part moth. The question is, how?"

"What is 'stare'?" I ask. "It just happened. I don't think I control it."

"When we first met, you thought moths to be harbingers of doom. Some of that rumor begins with legends of seeing one's own doom in the eyes of the mothman. In short, their guilt drives them to paranoia. Paranoia drives them to penance," Phorbas vaguely explains before continuing in a more cheery tone. "Of course, I have heard only a handful of tales such as this. Yours is the first whose legitimacy I believe, seeing as you have no prior knowledge of the legend and thus could not be lying. Deduction would say not all moths have this capability, or it would say most creatures face to face do not have the depths of evil required to enact it."

"Well, if I can't practice *staring,* and I can't practice being in a fight or flight response, what are we going to work on?" the pupil requests of the sensei.

"In every scenario, I have noticed that your control, your attitude, was always the greatest enemy. With the sasquatch, you were angry. With Yatee, you were consigned over to death. With Ellie, you were forced to fight or die," Phorbas seems to be reading off his case file of me. "Our tongues and our temper are the two most difficult beasts to tame in all of the world. I will not pretend to have fully mastered mine, but we must address yours with haste."

He acts like he isn't the most level-headed person I know. He doesn't curse, and he's never lashed out at me. I think he's got his beasts pretty well-tamed.

"Allow me to tell you a story," Phorbas continues, "of a lost man who desperately needed guidance, who desperately needed his inner beasts tamed."

He weaves a web about a girl taken from the moth village. When mothmen are young, they are not larvae like the moth insects. They are somewhat humanoid, small, and defenseless, much like human children. They have no wings and no talons and rely on their colony for protection. When children have reached their teenage equivalent years, they enter into an egg-like cocoon — more similar to what we know to be a chrysalis.

When they emerge from this chrysalis weeks later, their bodies have grown to maturity. They have wings to spread and claws to sharpen. This incubator, being fueled by radiation, causes rapid and expansive physical growth. When the moth-man emerges, however, their mind is still very much immature and in need of molding. The older and, thus, wiser moths take in the young hatchlings to help acclimate them to the harsh outside world as quickly as they can.

Moths without a mentor rarely live beyond a year. If they hatch and refuse to listen, they can fly as far as their hopes will carry them and will not be prepared for the reality that awaits them on the ground.

Phorbas was meant to serve as a mentor to the young girl who was taken. Moths form their own cocoons wherever they choose: on the underside of giant leaves, holes in large oak stumps, or slimy caves. They are not bound to the safety of the village, but the elders are expected to locate and watch over them while they metamorphize.

One night, while Phorbas was checking in on all of the pods, he noticed one was gone. No remnants of hatching, no husk, no shell, all of it was gone. Something or someone had taken the entire egg-like structure. A predator would have dug in, eaten the creature inside, and moved on. This was not that; the entire thing was missing.

"We had never seen anything like that before," Phorbas says, looking more grim than a winter sky. "Kidnapping is not a crime committed by beasts. What use does a carnivore have for a hatchling other than to costume it?"

"That egg was taken then. You think it was hiders," I try to jump ahead in the depressing story. He does not indulge me.

"Eliminate the impossible. Whatever remains must be the truth," Phorbas says. "That was the unfortunate first lesson I learned as a detective. The next was that sometimes a trail goes cold. And stubbornly pursuing a cold trail will turn you cold right along with it."

He goes on to tell me how the guilt weighed on him. How he thought every pair of glowing eyes he saw was casting judgment on him. His village maintained that they wanted to embrace him, but he wouldn't let himself receive forgiveness. He thought his mistake should make him an outcast, but he later realized that his brazenness only resulted in his people losing two moths instead of one. They operate similarly to humans, but not entirely. Protecting the young is a top priority, but elders and their knowledge are often viewed as just as important in preparing for the future.

His time in self-isolation was dark. At one point, Walking Sam was the only voice he had heard for days. Phorbas never admitted to the depression, but he isn't the only one of us too

CHAPTER 16

proud to open up about it. Hearing all of this made me wonder. Phorbas was already an elder before this disaster. Wasn't he wise, then? How could a wise man fall into despair like that? Doesn't time make you immune to being stupid or something?

"Didn't you know better than to spiral like that?" I ask. "You were going to be that girl's mentor after all, right?"

"Yes, yes. Wise enough to know better, yet prideful enough to think it would not apply to my circumstance," he exhales like chains have fallen off his wrists. "Truth be told, I was angry. Both at myself and at some unseen force that had caused it all."

"What changed? How did ya pull yourself out?"

"I did not. A hand reached in after me. Sometimes, it takes the help of a friend to remind us of who we are. Not the lower version we think ourselves to be. Geiger is your best friend, and I can see why she would do anything to help you. And for what it's worth, I would, too."

Thinking about people caring for me has always been tricky. Part of me feels like that makes me a burden, and the other part of me thinks that's too close for anyone to be. I ask the first thing that comes to mind to sprint away from that feeling.

"Is your friend still around?"

His faint grin tells me there is no sadness associated. "He is. And it so happens that he is in need of a little help from a friend. You will meet him once I have repaid his favor to me." Phorbas ends the campfire tale and pats my shoulder. "For now, however, there is work to be done."

I don't immediately follow his lead. I sit a moment longer, and he asks what I'm thinking.

"Do you think people can change? I don't mean outwardly like me and the other lab rats. Do you think I can actually change who I am?"

"Who we are is determined by our actions. If you feel the need to change, there is nothing more to do than change your decisions. Change your reaction from rage to gentleness, change your words from toxin to tea," Phorbas speaks tenderly. "I do love tea," he fancily adds with a smack on my back.

"Ow."

"Come now, let's get going."

We set our course toward the town of Kelly. I have a feeling it will be a good day.

17

Chapter 17

Walking and talking is our number one hobby at this point. Not really caring anymore why Phorbas asked me to come to the Spikes, he went ahead and explained to me how I could bridge the two worlds and how I could appeal to the scientists who were conducting horrible tests on sentient intelligent beings. I told him that was a no-brainer. Our goal now should be getting to the foundation and freeing any creatures still being held unfairly. The teleporter is our obvious and quickest way in, but the only person who knows how to work the thing ate half my shoulder for lunch yesterday. So, I guess step one is seeing where her mind is at.

We exit the cover of the forest and see the eerily homey junkyard wall of garbage. A night in the woods will make any shelter seem like a refuge. Phorbas stands up straight and puts his arm like a bar across my chest.

"Do you hear that?" he asks me.

He motions me to walk lower and slower. The closer we get to the wall, the more I hear what he must have heard. It's a radio of some kind, maybe? We inch closer and closer, and the sound becomes clearer.

"*RUN LIKE HELL *tzzkt* RUN LIKE HELL *tzzkt**" plays over and over again like the tape is stuck.

"Geiger..?" I look to Phorbas. His eyes tell me something is not right.

"His dog is here, Dr. Fowler. So, he must not be far behind. Where have you hidden him?" a mystery voice interrogates Ellie. A loud thud sounds after a second of her silence. Then, an outburst, "Tell me!"

I shove my eye into a hole in the fence of garbage. It's Dr. Hyde. Ellie looks beaten, which is partially my fault, but he has added fresh wounds to her. Geiger is lying near their feet. She is incapacitated. One of her eyes is not illuminated, and one of her legs is twitching. The static of her recording continues to play. My poor girl. We'll get you fixed up after this, I promise.

"Let's kill those bastards," I jerk my spine to stand, but Phorbas holds me down.

"Patience. We must build a plan together."

As much as I'd prefer to fly off the handle and hope the moth in me makes another appearance, he's right. If I mounted this gate, I'd be tazed by a hundred different sources of current before I even touched Dr. Hyde. We look through the peepholes a little longer. There are at least four hiders, excluding the doctor himself. They appear to be clean-up crew muscle as they all are toting sheathed shock batons.

"This isn't working," Dr. Hyde sighs and strikes the back of his hand across Ellie's face. "Bring her through."

A crew member motions to another who is working a console inside the shed. After a few key clacks, the teleporter platform begins to hum. A tiny blue circle appears above the platform. The circle is expanding by the second. It is not a sphere. It is

CHAPTER 17

a flat circle within the jutting arch. As it expands I can see lab equipment and familiar fluorescent bulbs. The room must be at the Foundation, though I have never seen this room. The whirring circle expands to the floor until it is large enough for a yeti to pass through.

On the other side, a masked hider is grabbing at someone. It's Mom. Her hands are bound, but she is not resisting their force. Her face looks stoic like being here is an annoyance. It reminds me of a face I would make when I knew I was upset and there was nothing anyone could do to change it. She steps through the ring of teleporter light. Her dark hair washes forward as the sending gate closes behind her.

"Call to him, Carpenter," Dr. Hyde commands.

"He's not your pet. He's my son," Mom combats him.

"Wrong. My research saved him by *your* choice. You *chose* to make him mine."

Mom rolls her eyes. She knows he won't hurt her. The twine wrapped around her wrists is a glorified formality. They want to invoke anger from me and make me act on emotion, as usual. If I didn't know any better, I'd say Mom is trying to keep her cool so that I keep mine.

"You know he heals. That's why he can be out here so long," Mom implies their reason for following me.

"Dr. Fowler heals, too. Look at her grotesque mug," Dr. Hyde points to Ellie. "If the radiation is changing him, I deserve to study that."

"Eric was exposed to his treatment when he was a boy. His body grew with it, adapted at every developmental cycle," Mom appeals. "Whatever is helping him can't help you. You've already tried splicing yourse—" Mom's plea is stifled with a kick to the back of her knee. She falls to the ground and looks

133

over her shoulder at the masked muscle man, "Really?"

"Call him, Carpenter. Now." Dr. Hyde squares his shoulders even with his convictions.

The crew member standing behind Mom unsheathes his baton. The initial crackle of the hot electricity makes her jump. Mom closes her eyes and takes a deep breath.

"Eric," she raises her voice. "If you can hear me, if you're hiding, you probably want to do something crazy right about now. From the bottom of my heart, don't. Run. Run so far they will never find you."

Phorbas turns to me and says, "Run east."

I look at him, confused. I can't just run.

"Run east," he says to me again. "I have a contingency plan. While they chase after you, I will help your friends."

Not giving me a second to respond, Phorbas lets out a guttural call.

"What was that? He's hiding behind the fence," I hear the chatter of hiders.

"Now would be a proper time, trust me, brother," Phorbas pleads.

Calling out over our trashy line of defense, I yell, "I hope you're faster than ya look, fatass."

I sprint toward the eastern tree line. The fence clangs as the hiders topple their beer guts over the wall. The flashlights in their hands smack the top bar of the fence and remind me of my advantage. I will run as Phorbas instructed, but if I am forced to fight, they'll never see me coming.

Before I enter the woods, I look back to make sure Mom sees me. I want her to know I'm okay, and I want to know that she's okay. I give her a half-smirk smile, but she does not return it. As confident as she is in me, she is still my mom, and her worry has painted her face ghostly pale. Dr. Hyde is pulling her arm back through the teleporter's ring. If this is the last time I see her, I'm sorry to have made her look so scared.

This forest is not quiet. The boots of my pursuers splash mud with every step like a stampede. The lights from their torches are shakily bobbing around my outline and desperately trying not to lose me. Not that I want to be transforming into a moth, but some midnight sky black fur would be nice right about now.

Ideas are swirling in my mind. Phorbas' command of 'run east' was rather vague. Did he mean forever? Until I hit the Glowing Sea? His instructions were to run, not to think, and not to fight. Behind me, all around me, is the blue light of crackling bolas illuminating the forest floor. They're *actually* throwing those things at me. Feeling like a dart board with legs is not a fun time. I owe a lot of cryptids an apology.

A sting of pain shocks my body. My limbs seize, my left hand contorts, and I hit the ground in a crumble. One of them managed to hit me. The shock is like a light switch, on one second and off the next. If I gather myself quickly enough, maybe I can run again. In front of me is a thick tree trunk. I dig my elbow into the dirt to try and drag myself behind it before they catch up to me. It didn't take an expert tracker to follow the snail-like trail I left in the mud. It's not long before a blinding torch points down at me.

"Over here, we got him," a hider calls to his compatriots. "Huh? What is — *AHH!*"

In a fading holler, he is yanked out of my sight. His torch falls from above and hits the ground in front of me. I stare at it for a moment, trying to guess what I witnessed. The ground feels like it's about to rupture. A roar sounds from the dirt beneath me, and I hear the other hiders panicking. This familiar chaos is like music to my ears. A soft yellow glow surrounds the tree as an eye opens from its splintering center.

"Yatee!" I exclaim. "You big beautiful birch."

"*There will be more. You must run. Screams will not end until I am done.*"

Yatee's branches cut the cool night air like whips. Vines crack out to lace the back of another hider. Bolas begin filling the air like lightning bugs. Wood of course does not conduct electricity, the hiders have met their match. Bolas fall around me after their zaps knock against Yatee's trunk.

I am still trying to gain feeling in my fingers from my shock treatment. A hider uses her shock baton to smack approaching vines and branches away. Yatee's canopy is deceptively large. A branch sneaks behind and knocks the hider up into the sky. Her shout of fear grows distant, then close again. She slams on the ground in front of me. The pop of her contorted limbs breaking on impact almost masks the yells of the petrified filling the woods around me.

Finally wiggling my toes, I hop up. The base of Yatee's trunk seems as safe as anywhere, but I can't risk it. I yell up to announce my departure to Yatee. He is dangling his midnight snack down into his earthy gullet, so he pays me no mind. You can't catch anything running in a straight line unless you're faster than it, so I continue east. To what end? Maybe until I can no longer hear the carnage.

Overgrown plant leaves brush over my face as I blaze through uncharted territory. My shins have collected thin scrapes and wet dew from the half-mile of grass blades I've matted down on my trek. I'm not sure if he is full or if I've gone far enough away, but I do not hear any more cries from Yatee's direction.

It feels safe to rest. I've only had a few days away from the track at the Foundation and can tell my cardio is not what it should be. There is a downed log beneath a break in the forest's ceiling where the moonlight is shining through. I plop onto the makeshift bench in a heap. My hair is sticky from sweat, and my legs are covered in grass clippings. I held up my end of the plan with Phorbas, but now I am worrying about his end. Was he able to help Mom, or are they both bound and going to be used as hybrid moth bait?

Something pulls my head to the side like a string is attached to my chin. I am facing my newly minted path. What was that? I didn't hear anything; at least, I don't think I did. A survival reflex, maybe? Is my body trying to show me something? I lean on the log until my body weight is resting fully on my elbow. Staring as hard as beast eyes can stare, I don't see anything. My chin tugs to the right, nearly spinning my head around. Okay, I heard something that time.

Resting like an idiot, I should've kept running. Whether it's a baton-wielding middle-aged man or a creature with four rows of jagged teeth, I can feel something stalking around me. Even with better night vision, my eyes have adjusted to the brightness of the moon, making things within the darkened canopy hard to see. Into the light, out of the shadow, there is a shape forming. A large and arduous shape. Its footfalls are nearly silent.

The moon first reveals a hand with two long claws, then a thick, hairy forearm like a primate might have. Stepping better into view, the shoulder of the creature has human skin, and its face is entirely human, with sunken, unwavering eyes hidden behind a glass breathing apparatus that covers his whole face. What steroid shot in the ass could have possibly doubled his arm count? His four-armed torso makes it impossible to buy comfortable sweaters; I just know it. This abomination looks as if you were trying to pull a human out of the back of a giant sloth. The core is man, but the extremities are nothing close. His spine is slightly too long, and his legs are suspiciously too tall. Whatever this beast is, he is an experiment like me.

"Aren't you a little too old for trick-or-treating?" I insult.

"Make this easy. Come with me." He replies in a rehearsed, albeit human, voice.

"Yeah, no thanks." I try to run, but he jolts after me and blocks my path with his anchor-like arms.

"I'll catch you if you run," the beast states. "I'll kill you if you fight. I'm bringing you into the Foundation one way or another."

His expression reads like misery. Is his form causing him pain? My vision is turning red again. My body didn't respond this quickly to Ellie. The danger this monstrosity poses must be more evident. I try to get off my starting block fast, but the moment my heels turn to run, the beast swings his sledge-like hands and knocks my feet out from under me.

"Last chance, 001."

"How do all of you know me? I've never heard of any of you!"

"They'll answer questions at the Foundation," his neck twitches as he speaks.

Laying flat on my back, staring up at a nearly ten-foot-tall behemoth, a feeling of defeat washes over me. No fight, no flight, just frozen. Maybe I could feign defeat and make a run for it. Maybe I could fight, try to break his breathing mask, and hope sleep spore saves me again. Those plans are fading ideals. What help would I be to Phorbas if this thing broke me in two or if they never gave up their pursuit? Living to fight another day is my only option.

The creature motions in the direction I ought to go. I rise to

CHAPTER 17

my feet with my hands in the air like a caught thief. He grabs my shoulder, and the edge of his claws wraps down to my scapula. Before I can react, his lower-row hand juts a syringe and injects a mystery concoction into my gut. The red haze of night grows fainter until my vision is black entirely.

Chapter 18

At first, it felt good to be lying down. That is until I remembered what had put me to sleep. I pop up like waking from a nightmare. The white fluorescent bulbs nearly blinded me when my eyes slammed open. Blocky computers and hand restraints tell me exactly where I am: the Foundation.

From the back corner of my holding cell, I don't know what floor I'm on or if this is a floor I would recognize either way. This could be minus-one, or it could be somewhere new entirely. Mom is in here with me. Her hands are bound, but she is free to walk around. I, however, am latched to a vertical gurney of sorts. Ellie might have warned them that I could fly off the handle if the need arose.

"You're awake," Mom walks over to my bedside.

"What was that thing?"

She shakes her head. "Wollston has been playing with mutagens again. That abomination he sent after you could be anybody, someone disposable, I'm sure."

Mom put the backside of her hand up to my forehead. She

knows full well I wasn't restrained because I had a fever. It must be a mom thing.

"How are you feeling?" she asks me.

"Not too bad," I keep my reply short and my eyes down.

It feels like there is an elephant in the room that only I can see. What does Mom know about my last few days? How does one smoothly dive into the whole, "So, about my moth genetics?"

I begin to speak, but the start of our sentences overlap. Mom nods at me to go first.

"What do you know?" my question comes out more trembly than expected.

"Everything, sweetie." She grabs my hand with her bound ones. "Dr. Fowler sent an alert that a seeker was beyond the Spikes and seemingly communicating with a mothman. When I heard that, I knew it had to be you."

"It's not just moths, ya know. I can talk to all of them. Well, all of them that talk anyways."

Her eyes widen, and her chin scrunches. "That is fascinating. You always have been."

I don't know if she's speaking as my mom or as a researcher. That's maybe the beginning of a new problem. Is she with me or with them?

"If you assume I know the story by now, I don't," I tell her. "I'm assuming I got a shot in the ass like the other freaks."

"Language." Mom scolds. Her eyes drop as she breathes out a sigh. "I should've never hid it from you. It was part embarrassment for me and part thinking I could somehow shield you from the gritty mess of this place."

It seems a lot like she fully thrust me *into* the gritty mess, but I keep that thought to myself.

"It happened that day, didn't it?" I ask. "With the ahool?"

141

"Yes, yes, it did." She turns her face away from me completely. "It's all my fault. Every last bit of it."

The collapsing door to our room spins open.

"Oh, don't blame yourself there, Gracious," Dr. Hyde boisterously announces his entrance. "Everything we have done here has led us one step closer to our greatest achievement: life everlasting."

He ends his grandiose speech with stifled coughs. The rad sickness rotting his organs needs to shit or get off the pot. Two researchers in surgeon masks follow in behind him. One makes their way behind my headboard and begins wheeling me out. The other stays with Mom.

"We're going on a field trip," Dr. Hyde says. "I have been dying to show little Eric his origin story for quite some time now."

They steer my hand truck-style gurney out into the hall. We pass several rooms with nothing but small windows on the doors. Most rooms appear empty, with the occasional brown-furred creature resting in them. We hit a large set of double doors that require Dr. Hyde to use a keycard to access them. Once his ID is accepted, the doors swing open to reveal a dimly lit workshop.

Green light glowing out of the computer monitors brightens every few feet of our path. Bright illuminated side rooms pour their white light out into the large workshop through what I am assuming are two-way mirrors. As I am wheeled past them, the creatures inside do not notice us, or maybe they no longer care. How long have any of them been here?

We then begin passing windows whose rooms hold humans and not beasts. Some humans look more acclimated than others. Some look nervous with no sign of foreign DNA, and others look at home with facial oddities and skeletal deformities. On the back wall of this expansive workshop is a single chamber.

We enter through its doors. Rows of servers and filing cabinets line the left side of the room. The right side could best be described as a hall of fame. Sections are roped off for experimental design prototypes, cryptid skeletons, and God knows what else.

"You've seen our teleporter in action," Hyde says. "What did you think?"

"I think you're too stupid to build something like that."

He jeers. "Right, you are. This was our first model," he says, looking toward a display of heaped metal. "It was a little unstable for our liking before your mother had the idea of linking the energies with a sender and a receiver. The things we sent through almost never ended up where we intended. Hence, the birth of you s*eekers.*"

"So everyone here cleans up your mess in some form or another."

He shakes his head like I'm his friend teasing him over old times gone by, "Most of you here *are* my mess." He continues to point at displays, including metal and string bolas from early human civilization, the skeleton of a large cryptid quadruped thought to be extinct, and something that resembles an egg. "Recognize her?" one eyebrow of his arches at me.

Silence is my reply. Something about it is familiar, though. It's like I recognize it but can't place where from.

"No? This beauty was your home for a week or two," he says. "Granted, you probably wouldn't remember that, given your state at the time."

It's an egg. Or at least that's what it looks like. It's old and nearly all wilted brown, despite the conservation efforts I'm sure he has employed trying to preserve yet another dying thing as long as he can.

My curiosity gives way. "That thing? How was that my home?"

Dr. Hyde smirks like he's won a prize. He's the elder brother who knows all the family secrets and dangles that forbidden fruit of knowledge in front of my face. "This is your *chrysalis* if you will. It wasn't fully yours, of course. It belonged to me, and my research, to the Foundation." He brushes his hand over the egg's exterior like they are sharing fond memories. "Your mother, dear, dear friend of mine she was, commandeered it from me."

"Mom stole your egg? Get to the point shi—"

"She thought it was the only way to save you. I told her to let you go, but that just made her even more hysterical. So, being the friend that I am, I let her use my property to save your life." He turns his attention back to me with a smug look on his face. "Removing the moth larva herself, she thrust you into the egg sack center. No guarantees that you would survive. I thought she was insane, if I'm honest, but genius rarely is. Sane, of course."

"A moth chrysalis. That's why I can—"

Dr. Hyde interrupts me again, "That's why you can heal, communicate with the beasts, change into glowing red eyes, and whatever other secret things you have managed to keep from me." He continues while pacing around the decrepit shell. "Your mother had told me about the healing. She had a suspicion about night vision — no proof, all anecdote, but she never once indicated anything *extraordinary*. Which was always typical of the men in her life." He looks at me, waiting for an outburst. I won't give him the satisfaction.

CHAPTER 18

Mom either never noticed anything extraordinary, or she kept it all a secret to protect me. Healing seems to be common enough, Ellie could do it after all. There was nothing new they could learn from me. For his intent, I wasn't all that useful. At least, not as an experiment; he used me in the seeking field for years. Maybe that was his bargain with Mom. He wouldn't throw me out with the trash, but we had to work to earn our keep.

"That radiation you've been exposing yourself to seems to have awakened more," Dr. Hyde is looking at me closely. "We noticed some silken scarring on your back. We will study that before too long. And Dr. Fowler indicated you had great strength and endurance. You rivaled her own with your beady red eyes," he lets out a quick laugh. "Dr. Fowler was scared shitless of you. And to think, you've had this potential under our noses the whole time. Why did we never try to force more out of you? Your mother has more sway on me than I realize, I'm sure."

"Slow down there, Wollston," his face twitches a bit when I call him by his first name. "The moth inside the egg, what happened to her?"

"Her? I don't believe I specified the sex. You really can talk to that moth, can't you?" He leans in like he's studying my face before he blabs on. "A larva removed halfway through its transformation is deformed. Until the metamorphosis is complete, the process cannot be interrupted. Splitting the chrysalis open sealed the little one's fate." Dr. Hyde puts his finger on my forehead. "But just to save you, your mother made that trade — the larva's life for yours."

My heart wants to break, but I'm not sure for which cause. Mom saved me. I suppose I should be grateful. But at the cost of another life, I don't think that was worth it. A moth peacefully undergoing her change into adulthood was murdered so that I could live. The same tragedy that sent Phorbas into his depressive spiral is the very one that ended up saving me. I can't change what happened, but I can make well enough sure they both get their vengeance.

"I always knew somethin' was up," I indulge the doctor's curiosity. "But I'd be lying if I said this is what I expected." I stare at the empty cocoon. It doesn't even look real, like something we were never meant to see.

"This chrysalis, this method of mutation, might be our key. All of the DNA splicing we have done, the serum injections, the radiation treatments; there are always adverse effects," he pauses and thinks a moment. "But you, you are different. All your life, you pass as a human until your body needs to respond. And wow, did it ever," he stares at my hair stripe. "I can't say I'd like to be shut up in a vacuum seal for a few weeks, but if it cures me, I suppose there isn't much of a choice."

Do they have another egg? If he has the means to carry out his own incubation, then maybe his body will rebuild itself, throwing out the bad and replacing it with good. If they don't have an egg, then finding one would be their top priority. How could they find one? They'd need a moth. Shit. They have Phorbas.

Grim thoughts haunt my mind. While I'm being paraded around the VIP tour, Phorbas is probably being tortured or fit with a tracking device and a shock collar. This place has been torturing cryptids for two decades; they must be good at it by now. He is smart enough to know that if they miraculously set him free, it's because he's leading them straight to the other moths.

CHAPTER 18

I'm the only one who can communicate with him, and surely they're not dumb enough to put him and me in a room and expect me to accurately translate what he's saying. Maybe they simply want to research him. To hiders, he is a legendary find. So much so that I was told my whole life that moths were myths and never confirmed. Another lie from them. I need to get back to Mom fast. Maybe she and I can get free and find Phorbas together before they do something irreparable.

"What happened to those?" I motion my head at the servers by the door. Some of the knowledge caches on the opposite end of the room appear to be burnt. Some of the floor tiles are scorched black, and the metal of the cabinets is warped.

Wollston's face turns the color of the rough end of a matchstick. He's looking at me like I asked the question with the purpose of annoying him. "Those were damaged in a fire." He studies me more. "Let's get you back to daycare. I'm sure Mommy misses you."

On my free ride back to the holding cell, I see him, Phorbas. He is in one of the large lab's offshoot rooms. The mirrors are one-way, but his eyes follow us all the way through. Tubes and wires are draped over his body. His wings and his arms are wrapped up tight in a straitjacket of sorts. Two hiders are in the room with him, checking his vitals on the nearest monitor. This may be the first moth they've had since the egg came through. They aren't missing an opportunity to learn everything they can. I know where he is now. I know where they're holding him; it's their first mistake. If I can get free, I can come back for him.

When the spinning cell door slides open, Mom looks at me with bloodshot eyes. She wears shame and guilt like it's eye shadow. What emotion is she expecting of me? My usual one-liner? Something fully condescending but only passively aggressive? Phorbas told me that if I want to change, truly change, and be someone I am proud to be, I have to change my decisions. Emotions are not always our decision, but how those emotions control our actions is always our choice.

"What did he say?" Mom asks.

I recap the history lesson he gave me. Getting through the story was nearly unbearable. Every word I spoke hammered my mother's shoulders lower and lower. She doesn't need to be so regretful, so ashamed. I'm here today because of her, and she did what any mother would've done. I don't blame her, but will she truly hear me when I say it?

"You shouldn't be so upset, Mom. I don't blame you."

"That whole day was chaos, and the night before, too. Nothing but madness, and I am so sorry. There's so much more I can be blamed for."

"You don't have to be sorry," I tell her. "Not to me."

She wipes tears from the tip of her nose. "I am sorry to you, but not just you. We have hurt so many here, and I thought I could change it. I thought I could hide you from it." She shrugs in defeat, "You see how that turned out."

"Dr. Hyde is to blame," I say. "Every evil coming from this place, every ounce of loyalty you feel to him, it all came from his lies and his ego."

Mom sniffles but doesn't raise her eyes to me.

"We can win today," I continue. "We couldn't win back then; everything was so far out of your control, but today, we can win."

"There's so much you don't know," Mom says. "Just promise me that I'll always be your momma and that you know I always did what I thought was best for you — not us, *you*."

"Of course I know that. Always." Seeing her like this is

shredding the fibers of my heart. We have to act fast so Phorbas doesn't lose any fingers or toes, and I don't lose any control of my tear ducts. "We can win today, Mom. We can. How do we get out of here?"

She breathes out one heavy breath. "We play to our advantage. Who do you think helped design these freaky-looking doors?" The smallest hint of a smile curls the corner of her lips.

Her hands are still bound, and she picks at a tile on the floor, but it's not a tile; it's a repair hatch. She reaches her hands in and makes a few exerting tugs. After the third or fourth yank, the door enters its default powerless state: open.

Can't keep a good Carpenter down.

19

Chapter 19

Mom is headed to see if she can find information on Geiger's whereabouts. She thinks that, even though she might be considered an enemy at this point, the clean-up crew would still bring Geiger in for repairs — she is company property, after all. My job is to get to Phorbas before they have a chance to 'study' him. I hear Mom's voice over and over in my head, "Find G. Grab the mothman. Get to the teleporter."

It won't be long before they realize we have escaped our holding. One advantage we have is that this level of the Foundation is so secret that there simply are not very many workers, and nearly everyone wears a mask. The net over my hair and the filter over my mouth and nose match the scrubs I found quite well. The best place to hide is in plain sight.

Mom told me she would check mission intake logs for Geiger, but if they left her in the Radlands, it's just as well, considering that's exactly where we plan on escaping to. Find G. Grab the mothman. Get to the teleporter.

Every labcoat I pass nods at me like I'm one of them. Some of them don't even give me that much acknowledgment. There is a downside of being top secret and super secure — people get complacent. This floor or level or wherever the hell we are is not very big. From my holding room, a right took us to the archive and specimen storehouse, and a left took Mom to the teleporter and intake bay. I guess keeping a secret this big is easier when you keep the blueprint small.

My ear is pressed up against the double doors that lead to where I saw Phorbas. If Dr. Hyde is in there, I should be able to hear his condescending tone. I hear nothing except footsteps approaching. I duck in behind the door and pray whoever comes out of there has tunnel vision. They throw the door open, and I let it swing as close to shut as time allows. I grab the handle on the backside to prevent it from latching. The passing hider is none the wiser.

Not wanting to take any chances, I keep low as I slither around the desks in the middle of this workshop until I am in front of the cell that held Phorbas. I poke my head up to look through and assess his situation.

There are two hiders in the room with him, but neither of them is Dr. Hyde. Me and Phorbas versus two guys with hot sticks; this will be a breeze. After one last survey of the cubicle horizon, I make my approach to the room. A few steps away from the door, I hear a loud "NO" coming from the room. When I look up, Phorbas shakes his head at me, and the two doctors look at him, confused and terrified.

Can he see through the one-way glass? Also, I thought those rooms were soundproof. He had to put a lot into that. I point at myself and raise an eyebrow at him. He nods his head up and down and motions it to the right. Maybe he's motioning me backward and to the right. It's hard to tell. I back up to the desk

I was taking shelter behind earlier and point at it. Again, he nods.

He must be looking for something on the desk. What is all this stuff? There's a label on this desk that has the number '03' written on it. I look up at the room in front of me and notice there is also a number '03' on the door. Each room must have its own dedicated console. I peck the clacky textile keys and wait for the CRT monitor to flash on. Of course, it's password protected. Maybe something around here will give me a hint. I begin pulling out drawers and searching for secret sticky notes. Nothing that looks like a password sticks out to me, but on the underside of the desk is a red button with a small glass box over it.

I contort my neck to try and get a better look. There is no label to indicate what pushing this might do, but as a man with nothing to lose, that's exactly what I plan to do. When the button presses beneath my finger, I half expect an alarm to sound, but there is none.

I pop my head up to check on Phorbas. I need to make sure I didn't accidentally incinerate everything in that room. The guards are scrambling to the door, but it must be locked. They are grabbing at the door handle and trying to climb over one another to get out. Phorbas is still restrained, so what are they running from? The clawing of their hands slowly fades down the window of the door until they disappear completely.

I run up to the door and look through the window. Their bodies are lying stacked up against the door. Putting my shoulder into it, I force the door open. Pushing inch by inch, I manage to force a gap wide enough to fit through.

"Don't bother getting up," I tease at the restrained mothman, "I got it."

CHAPTER 19

Phorbas chortles. "They put me in a straitjacket — feels a bit unnecessary. You didn't tell them I was a gentleman of high cordiality?"

Squeezing through the door frame, I make my way over to him. I fidget around with his restraints before finding a hydraulic release.

"Did that button put some kind of gas in the air or somethin'?"

"Indeed," Phorbas says. "Meant to quell ornery patients but does not quite work on we creatures of the night that spew our own pathogens."

I'm happy to see him unharmed, but guilt is sneaking up on me. Not able to look him in the eye, I begin my explanation.

"Hey, listen, about your missing moth girl, I—"

"I know, brother." Phorbas cuts me off.

"It wasn't my choice," my eyes can't even direct toward him. "I would never have made that trade if—" A hug stops my blabbering.

He has odd, thin limbs, and his shirt smells like stagnant rainwater, but it is still comforting.

"Let not your heart be troubled, brother," he says. "There is no going back. We must move forward."

He breaks his embrace of me, and we turn to face the unconscious hiders.

"How did you know about that button on the desk?" I ask.

"Hiders study us, we study back. Come, one more lever to pull before we all make our escape."

We begin searching the main room for an emergency release that will open all of the holding cells. There are too many to go door to door with; we can't have much more time before they notice Mom and I are free.

As the thought crosses my mind, red lights flash like neon around the room. A robotic voice sounds over the intercom. "UNAUTHORIZED TRANSPORT ACTIVATED - UNAUTHORIZED TRANSPORT ACTIVATED."

Phorbas and I look at one another. That must be Mom. We need to hurry. I pound up the stairs to check the second level of rooms. Does each level have its own master release? If I can find one up here where there's less clutter, then maybe that will help us locate the one on the main level. I grab the latch of every door as I pass, but it seems the alert has locked all of the cells. Only the manual master release will free them now.

That stupid alarm is splitting my head. It plays over and over with no reprieve. The frustration of it all is enough to drive me mad, but I need to keep calm. I'm sure Phorbas is searching as well. I peer down over the metal railing to see where he's made it to. My heart sinks. I yell down to him.

"Phorbas! Turn around! Phorbas!"

Over this alarm, he can't hardly hear me. His head swivels to look my way, but it's too late. The four-armed abomination grabs his neck and hoists him into the air.

"Shit, shit, shit, shit," I sputter my way down the stairs.

As I turn to round the bottom step, I see it. Hanging like a pull chord from beneath the overhang is a red triangular handle. I look over to Phorbas, he is still hoisted high but facing the monster and from the looks of it giving him hell.

"I found it!" I yell, to no response.

I reach up and pull the cable, praying that it will be the right one. When I do, a sound like a clasping iron surrounds me and on the level above. A long beeping sound rings, and one by one, the doors of the cells fly open. Willing participants, captured cryptids, and anything in between are all free now. A cluster of fur bursts out of their holding cells like the hatch on the ark has been let down for the first time in forty days and blitz toward the double doors that lead into the hallway. None of them stop to help Phorbas. The stampede of mangled mongrels and altered animals bat the two of the combatants around. Phorbas flies above the crowd to avoid further hits. He scans the room and locks eyes with me.

"Follow them, brother! I will wrap things up here."

As he is trying to embolden my confidence in him, I see the giant sloth half-breed rise from the sea of beasts like a shark hunting seals. He swipes his clawed mitt up and swats Phorbas out of the sky like an unwanted pest. The mothman crashes down through a research table below. Following in behind the crowd of cryptids, I rush over to him.

"Are you okay?" I ask Phorbas. "Get up, we can take him."

The behemoth is swimming his way up a stream of monsters, giving us time to form a plan.

"You must go. I will handle this alone." Phorbas grits as he rises to his feet.

"What happened to 'let people in,' 'do not go it alone'?!" I ask. "I'm not leaving you. Two moths are better than one."

Phorbas grabs my forearm but never takes his eyes off the pursuing beast. "You are not a moth, not in your current state. You have a fight of your own. Give me this one."

"Maybe if he hits me a time or two, my fight response will kick back in," I argue. "I'm not about to leave you here."

"The activation of the teleporter triggered the alarm. Everyone in this facility was alerted like a homing beacon, like a porch light in the dark." Finally, he looks at me with a deep dread only a legendary mothman can sustain. "Your mother needs you more than I. You are her light worth dying for. Don't let her."

As much as I can't stand it, he's right. Mom might have Geiger, but the last time I saw her, she was in no condition to help defend anyone. I've gotta get past this guy and get to her. The swarm of angry test subjects has probably paved an easy enough path. I nod to Phorbas. We understand it must be this way.

We charge the amalgamation. He squats his legs to brace for a tackle. Phorbas goes high and meets his four hands in a lock. I slide under his legs and sprint for the door. The groaning and pains of a fistfight are hard to ignore. Even if Phorbas uses his wings to his advantage, the beast will always overpower him.

Reaching into my pocket, I decide to leave Phorbas a little help. The plastic ball warbles blue at its edges. My arm winds up a pitch. The bola splits mid-air and sails on target. A hot strike of lightning cracks out. A direct hit to the back of the monster's neck. Phorbas, hovering over the distracted screaming creature, gives me a wave. He dive bombs on top of the beast as I nod what could be my last goodbye to my moth friend. Running around the corner of the hall, the double doors now blown off their hinges, the last thing I see is that crooked, spiky smile. That horrible, crooked, spiky smile. My friend is going to be just fine.

Chapter 20

This hallway floor is cobbled with hoof prints, and the walls are painted with horn scratches. The stampede we set free made a break for the loading bay. If I didn't know the way, I could follow the animal fur, feathers, and smell of blood. Several offshoot rooms, like the one they kept me and Mom in, have their doors blown open from blunt force. After looking inside to examine one too many, I stopped checking the rooms for survivors. I do not know the crimes the hiders committed here, but if the punishment from these beasts equals the crime, it must've been truly dreadful.

The alarms are still sounding. I follow the path of dirt and grime to the double doors of the bay. These doors are blown off their hinges like all the others before them. I hear the crackling sounds of destroyed electrical equipment. Between the bursts of red light from the alarm is a blue pulse of light from the teleporter.

I poke my head inside the door frame to assess the carnage. Flares of popping electricity fly from busted CRT monitors. Tape from trampled research cartridges is scattered over the floor. The red and blue lights are matched by a single swinging hanging light that still has its power. The room is small and intimate. A stage of consoles and monitors overlooks a flat showroom that houses the teleporter ring. Surrounding the ring are four or five workstations that can view the miracle technology from every angle.

"Eric?" a voice calls from my left.

Mom is slouched in a heap on the floor, and a thin blood trail draws a line down her forehead. Geiger is with her.

"G! You're okay!" I say.

"Hard to keep a good Carpenter down," she replies. "This Carpenter, however, is not feeling her best." Geiger gestures toward Mom.

I kneel to check on her. When my hand brushes her hair to look at her cut, Mom swipes my hand away.

"I'm fine," she says. "We have work to do. We can slap a bandage on me later."

Geiger gives me a nod. She's already triaged Mom, and her approval makes me comfortable with continuing.

"Where's Hyde?" I ask.

Mom points to the glowing blue ring. "He went through. Ran like a scared puppy when he heard that herd running this way."

"We have to follow him. Can't let him escape now," I say with a jerk upward of my shoulders.

Mom grabs my wrist to stop me. This also stops Geiger, who was ready to follow my lead. "Wait. Wollston has been keeping mutagen vials that yielded potentially beneficial results. He kept them all in a black box. I was able to keep him from using the mutagens on himself for a while," Mom shakes her head, "but when he went through, he had the box with him."

"You think he might," I begin, but she cuts off my thought.

CHAPTER 20

"He's not who he used to be. The man who started this foundation has been gone a long time. I used to think I knew what he would and wouldn't do, but now—"

From the middle of the room, I hear a noise tearing and popping. Someone is coming through the ring. A giant hairy shoulder reveals itself. Then, a veiny bulging head. The face belongs to Dr. Hyde, but I'm not certain the body belongs to him.

"Don't get up, Dr. Gracious. " He wheezes between breaths. I'll let myself in."

His breathing is labored, and he isn't moving fast. His bones are likely still setting into his new frame.

"What do we do?" I ask.

My resolve is panicked. But Mom is unwavering like the wind against redwoods.

"We need to get to the console on the other side," Mom instructs. "I hate to tell you this, but everything's gonna be okay. Remember that."

"Of course, I know that," I lie to her face. "What's my job?"

"You gotta distract him."

"Ah, that's where the hope speech came from, huh?"

"Son, you can do this. The radiation leaks through the teleporter. I'm grabbing a rad suit, and we will sneak past you two. Two minutes at the most," she assures me, but I do not feel assured.

Geiger extends me a fist bump. Whatever patching Mom did to her, she needs to take another look. "I believe in you. I will be just on the other side if you need me."

"Wow, how thoughtful of you," I reply.

I begin to get up and face the creature that is now wholly through the ring. Again, Mom stops me.

"When I tell you to leave and get to the other side, you do it. Hastily. And I don't mean maybe, do you hear me?" Mom asks. Her voice is stern, but her eyes are soft.

"I hear ya, Mom. I'll be there. No matter what."

"*THEY CAN REBUILD YOU. NOT ME,*" Geiger plays.

"I hear you too. I'll be fine, you guys. See ya in the rads."

Making my third and final attempt to attend to the matter at hand, a hand interrupts me. This time, it is on my shoulder, and the fingers on this hand eclipse my chest. The vast, beastly grip of Dr. Hyde squeezes me until something pops.

"Am I interrupting the kumbaya?" He lets out a horrid choking laugh.

Before I can react, he throws me across the room, down onto the flat level. The waxed floors squeal as my skin fights it for traction. Hyde leaps over the control console to pursue me. His head stands at the height of the console, and he's taller than before. Syringe vials hang out of his right thigh — some planted deep, others are half empty and dangling by a needle prick. Changes to his body are occurring in front of my eyes. There's no way to know what all he took. He is monstrous. I can see pulsing veins from his forehead to his shins applying pressure on his skin. His teeth have grown enlarged, and his legs have become digitigrade. I cannot imagine the pain his body is in.

"001. Alpha meets Omega," Dr. Hyde says.

He takes two steps on his front toes toward me and my neck hair reaches for the ceiling. I've fought bigger before, but those fights mostly consisted of outrunning. Even still, my advantage must be my speed. Moth DNA, don't fail me now.

Neglecting the fear inside me, I sprint at him. If I hope to survive this encounter, I'll need to learn as much as I can as

CHAPTER 20

early as possible. He should be lumbering; let's see how he keeps up.

He does not charge back at me. Instead, he draws his fist back and prepares for a punch. I slip under his log of an arm as it flings forward above my head. My left jab loads up and fires at his rib cage. Before it can make contact, his knee sends a piercing pain up my side. In his furious state of transformation, he is still swift enough to counter my counter.

Hyde capitalizes on my flinch and grabs my arm. He spins and sends me flying through the teleportation ring like a shot put. The air changes from cold and conditioned to hot and muggy. My face skids me to a stop in the dirt of the Kelly junkyard. The behemoth charges through the ring at me, led by his bolder-sized shoulder. One arm is now larger than the other, and his body leans forward from the weight of it.

I elevate myself and deflect over his head like a movie star survives an oncoming automobile. A red film begins to cover my eyes.

"Finally," I whisper to myself.

"I should leave you here with the trash," Dr. Hyde calls out. "Your study is no longer needed. I am become the penultimate beast."

His hubris takes a pause when he sees my eyes.

"Is that all you got? To think we wanted to learn anything of value from you. Red-tinted goggles are not quite the scientific discovery I was needing," a laugh gargles out of him.

"The eyes are just the windows," I say. "Wait till you get the full picture."

I discard the shirt of my hider disguise. My shoulders, and a taper from my obliques down to my hips, have grown thick black and purple fur. What's that for? Maybe just for show.

161

Either way, the more transformation and the more the moth takes over, the better my chances of survival.

My fists are raised like I know what I'm doing. I'll wait for him to make the next move. He's confident in his strength against mine. The one thing he has forgotten to account for is his loneliness. While we dance the waltz, Mom and G are shutting off access to his lab for good. There's been no sign of Phorbas yet; God, I pray he's safe. By any account, I have strength in numbers.

Dust shuffles into the air under the weight of his claws scratching up dirt as he runs. His movement is awkward. The weight of his upper body quickly outpaces what his legs can support, so I'll have to find any advantage I can. A giant arm extends over his head to strike down at me. I sweep sideways to dodge the blow. His other sledge tries to counter, but I duck under it and send a ripple up his abdomen with a swift punch.

That strength felt good.

He folds over in recoil, allowing me another attack opportunity. Another swift jab connects to his temple. His giant paw swipes faster than I can calculate, and he connects with his swipe to my face. With that same swipe, he strikes a backhand hit that sends me flying back through the ring and into the lab.

I brace my back for impact on the steel stage, but there is none. The silk bandages on my back are still there, I had almost forgotten. If they're nothing more than airbags cushioning my landings, I'd say they earned their purpose today.

Mom follows me through. I hadn't realized she and Geiger had already left the lab to begin with.

"What are you doing here?" I ask her. "This is the bad side, remember?"

"Geiger can pump energy from that side, but the main

controller is here," she says.

"No heroes today, Mom. When it's ready to blow, we are outta here."

She doesn't reply straight away. She's thinking. "I helped build this thing. Trust me."

Before I can petition her, a growl interrupts us. Hyde has followed me into the lab. If we are gonna cage this beast, I've got to keep him here on this side of the portal while we seal this sending gate shut for good.

"You must not have read the side effects label on that stuff," I taunt the beast.

"I created the effects," he gurgles out, "intended or not. I know them well."

"So you planned on being this ugly?"

He reaches down at me, but I grab his wrist and twist. If he doesn't follow my throw, his bones will snap. I hoist my body upward into his ribs and leverage his arm over my shoulder. In one gutting toss, using a great deal of my strength, Hyde flips over me, head first and flat on his back. I've got the behemoth on the ground.

My knee drives straight into his chest. I know I've got to keep him down as best I can. If he gets up, he's gonna be pissed. If I deny his feet footing and deny his momentum from swinging, I can keep him down with my body weight.

His arms swipe at me, and I deter them. A noise in my ear draws my attention. It's Geiger warbling on the other side. Her core is spinning up. She doesn't need much more time.

Dr. Hyde begins to cough. The cough smoothens and sounds more like a scoff.

"Good trick, boy. Want to see another?"

In my distraction, he attaches his palm to my throat like they are opposite ends of a magnet. My hands claw at him, but his arms are like velvet-covered steel. My bones pop as he rises to his feet, carrying me like a ragdoll in his grip.

"Your father had a smart mouth, too," the beast says. "Look where it got him."

What is he saying? I can barely breathe.

"Ahool have attacked one human structure in the history of our known universe. Don't play coy," he says, raising me to his eye line. He sees the confusion painted on my face. "She never told you?"

I'm sick of his cackling, but that doesn't stop him from reveling in his muck and bursting aloud.

"Your mother went on a subject hunt the night before the attack," he says. "The poor dear worked so late that she went straight from work to your little Sunday worship. We did not know then how astute the ahool sense of smell was. They followed her all the way home. Tell him, Grace! Tell your son of your failure!"

His voice changes as he speaks. He delights in the torture of his body, and like Ellie, his voice becomes less his own the longer he speaks. Thus far, we've kept it cordial. This fight has been mostly gentlemanly exchanges, but as the black syrup clouds his iris, I know that time is running short. Soon, this fight of men will be a fight of beasts.

"I thought that day would ruin me," Dr. Hyde continues. "But seeing those monsters' power and prowess let me know that I was on the right path."

My fingers burn as my digits have rashes from clawing so hard. My face and my temper are burning red. If looks could kill, I'd study him under a microscope. I can feel something is changing, but I don't know what. In a full metamorphosis,

CHAPTER 20

change is rapid.

Claws, antlers, somethings begin protruding from Hyde's arm toward his wrist. The bony growths are approaching my face. If I don't break free, they'll impale me. How can he stomach all this change at once? He acts like there is no pain, but there has to be.

"What is the old adage?" the monstrosity of Dr. Hyde asks me. "Break a few eggs to make an omelet? One hell of an omelet you turned out to be. Broken eggs, broken heads, broken families."

His neck wretches, and veins in his neck pulse with every heartbeat. My feet find footing pressed against his abdomen. With newfound leverage and his mind fleeing him more by the moment, I know this is my one shot to live. My bloodied fingers have destroyed and rebuilt themselves to reveal sharp claws. A slip in my step makes me notice my feet have done the same. I bury my front spurs into his torso. In each hand, I grab his wrist by the radius and ulna. My spiked hands penetrate his flesh until I can feel his dry bones in my palms. Using him like a launchpad, I explode his hand, splitting his arm in two down the center.

I land on my feet and await Newton's Third Law. His face lowers in a pained gurgle to meet my eyes. Nothing of the man I knew, who signed my paychecks, remains. Even the brow above his eyes has grown into a ridge. His eyes match the abyss of any angry animal I've seen before. Dr. Hyde has now completely succumbed to beasthood.

"NOW! Get out now!" I can barely hear Mom yell.

The warbling of Geiger's reactor and sparks flying from the teeming electrical stage make the air thick. An enormous amalgamated roar erupts from the abomination. The screams that make up this noise belong to no single creature. He sounds like a forest chorus. If he escapes into the wilds of the Radlands, nothing and no one will be safe. We must leave him stuck in this lab, a rat in a cage of his own design.

The flowing blood from his arm slows to a trickle. A jagged edge pops out to stop the bleeding. In replacement of his hand, a large spike has formed. Oh great, I took away one weapon, and the hydra grew another.

The amalgamation charges at me. Its bone appendage pings off the metal floor as his run matches the gallop of an ape. The beast leaps into the air and attempts to skewer me from above. The tip of the spear cuts my skin as I dodge him. My only advantages now are agility and an intelligent mind — not often I get the latter, but I'd better not waste it.

The end of his arm nearly penetrates the metal on impact. I land a few quick punches on his head that only aggravate him further. It screeches at me again. I slip under his paw as it swipes at me. My clawed foot feels the collapse of his ribs in a devastating kick. Unfortunately, in this fight of irradiated half-mutants, the little moments happen quickly and leave lasting effects. It felt good to crack his bones, but it did not feel good when his sword-like arm impaled me clean through my abdomen.

My eyes widen, and the crashing sounds silence themselves all around me. A million tiny receptors crying to heaven's gates, "This can't be happening to me." An expression I've gotten so used to that they may even write it on my headstone. *This can't be happening to me.* But it can, and it is, just like it always has. My father's death. My cracked skull. My mothman mentor. My cryptid DNA. Just as it always has, whatever *it* is, has always happened to me.

But damn it, I survive every time.

CHAPTER 20

I grit my teeth, throw my body's frame into the air, and remove myself from the skewer. I land on one knee and glance up at the creature. He is already pouncing into the air to prepare his killing blow. I am lightheaded, my organs are using every energy within me to repair themselves. I need to move and dodge, but I can't get out of the way in time. I lower my head to accept the hit, but it doesn't land. A gust of wind pulls me out of the way. The amalgamation's dagger pierces through the floor. Did Phorbas save me? What else could that have been?

I quickly survey the room to take inventory. Geiger is still glowing. Through my heavy blinking eyes, I see Mom pushing Phorbas away. She is really giving him a stern talking-to. Why does she look so afraid? Doesn't she know it's almost over?

My elbows quiver when I extend them to get up. My knees wobble when I finally reach my feet. A hand touches my back, and a mothy face yells at mine, though I can't really hear what he's saying.

Phorbas. Is he pointing at the portal or the fireworks show spewing from its edges? He pats my chest and takes flight to the blue ring. Bugs and their love for blue lights — unreal, he just can't help himself.

I can't even pretend to walk straight. My head hangs, rolling from one shoulder to the other. That fresh air feels good. I'm almost there. My feet stumble on fallen light fixtures and shattered glass that litter the floor. The sun no more than lights up my chin when I feel another hand. A larger, firmer hand.

The amalgamation, what's left of Dr. Hyde, grabs my forearm. He is tethered to the ground where his bone pierced the floor, and in his grip, I am tethered with him. I try to shake and struggle, but his resolve is unfazed by his injuries. Trapped raccoons gnaw off their limbs to survive, but I don't think I have that kinda time.

My friends, my team, stand like players on the sidelines. The ringing alarms drown out their coaching. The window to them is collapsing, smaller by the second. I turn to face the clutches of the beast. Spit drenches my face from his scream. I roll my eyes at the nausea of it all. My heel spurs dig into the grated floor. I fight for leverage, anything to break free from him again.

In his eyes, the ink clouds swirl like tempest waves. The frothing of the waters slows when his eyes meet mine, and a slideshow of horrors plays itself in my mind.

I see a catalog of beasts. Every beast I've ever seen, some I never have, they're all here in his memory. Sasquatch offspring being separated from their mothers. When the mother won't let them go quietly, he orders his men to put an end to her wailing.

I see Dr. Hyde on a boat manning a harpoon out on the Glowing Sea. The harpoon pierces air before it pierces the back of a sea serpent creature. The struggle between the prey and the fisherman causes the damage to magnify. The creature fights until the blue water is painted with red, like an artist washing their brush.

He is in his lab, watching over jackalopes. Every hour, he drops meat into their chamber and forces the herbivores to starve or adapt. Dr. Hyde thinks this experiment tests natural limits — are they real, or can they be ignored?

A dark night appears in my mind's eye. Led only by lamp lights, he places his hand on an egg-shaped chrysalis. He shines a light around it to observe the silhouette of the moth growing inside and motions for men to take it away.

I see through his eyes as he paws through a mound of rubble. His hands are bloodied, covered in splinters as he throws aside plank after plank of a fallen building. It takes all of his might, but he raises a final beam from its resting place. My father lay lifeless beneath it. In the curl of his body, under his arm, there I am. I see myself shielded from harm under my father's corpse. The vision blurs as Dr. Hyde screams for help.

Next, I see him alone in his office. He is staring at scans of his body. I don't know what they mean. But he feels sick, like his stomach may empty itself at any moment. Years of research beyond the Spikes and radiation exposure have rotted his vessel. He is afraid to die. So afraid that he will try anything to reverse the damage this line of work has inflicted on him.

My vision returns to my own. I can see not much of this doctor is left, but the eyes of this amalgamation do not show fear or regret. They express sorrow. The beast loosens his hold on me, but not completely. My backpedal moves me a few feet closer, I am barely hanging out of the lab and into the Rads before he loses his fight to the beast within.

A yank tussles me back. I can't give in. The ring of the sending gate is shrinking around me. I duck my head to make sure I'm not caught on the lip of its closing frame. My feet dig like digging has never dug before. An inch, I pull. Two inches, he pulls.

Dust blows in around me. There's that wind again. Where is it coming from? A swoosh of dust, followed by another, wafts in like a rhythm. The tempo increases the more my muscles flex.

My feet lose traction, and the dust fills the air around us. All I can see are the beast's jowls and bent brow. I feel light, weightless, like I'm flying.

Curiosity beats all logic, so I look over my shoulder. Wings are protruding from my back in the spots where I wore silk bandages. Even on the precipice of death, nothing can remove the smile that's growing on my face. I flap my wings harder. Each stroke gains strength like a whale preparing to breach the surface. A final warning sounds from the intercom, "*CRITICAL MASS.*"

My face is flush, and my palms sweat profusely. Every ounce of me is in this struggle. Phorbas grabs my pants by the belt loop and takes to the skies. Together, our power might be enough. The enclosing light ring passes the crown of my head, almost there, but the beast won't let me go.

"You blame me, but your mother caused it all," the *penultimate* beast screeches. "Your father, your mutation. She is the beginning of all this pain."

Harsh words would incur his wrath. But a soft answer might turn away his anger. "I don't blame you, Doctor," I say.

The eyes of the beast soften, the snarl of his jowl losing its coil.

"I forgive you," I say to him. He is a horrible, wretched monster, now both outside and in, but he wasn't always this way. "You didn't do it the right way, but you were scared. Scared of dying. Like you are now. We never know how we will act until the moment arrives. So, I forgive you. For it all."

The monster's eyes are white around the edges again. From his more human eyes, in a grotesque beastly form, tears streak down his face as he speaks, "You were never made to be an experiment. You were restoring her hope when there was none."

I look past his protruding shoulder. My mother is there on the stage behind him inside the lab. With tears in her resolved eyes.

She mouths to me, "I love you."

And from the top of my lungs and the bottom of my heart, I

CHAPTER 20

scream it back.

"I forgive her too," I tell the monster. "If there's even anything to forgive."

He looks back as the console reaches its brightest burn, and in a flash of light, an explosion sends a shockwave barreling toward us. The dust crashes out like waves. Shattered monitors and metal bits of the room once lying about hurl like debris.

The fierce air purges the beast from his pinned state. We both give way to the force. The ring of light seals in behind me as the eruption is locked in. A spherical hole, where the lab was moments ago, is carved in the sand, and my mother and the only lab entrance are gone.

My flesh burns, and one of my eyes cannot force itself open. I am lying flat in the dirt as blood creates a pool for me to float in. Shrapnel is littered around my chest and my legs. I cannot move my neck; my head rests to the side, seeing through a haze.

Through the clouds of dust, I see a hand still grasping my arm. A large mitt with veins butted up to the skin. My eye traces up the creature's arm. The arm connects to a bulbous ballooned shoulder. The shoulder connects to a face that is part beast and part Dr. Hyde. The face connects to nothing. It is sliced at an angle from one side of his brow down to the jaw of the other, all the way through, the perfect slice from a collapsed portal.

If I die here, if this is the end for the Carpenters, at least we took him with us.

There is a sharp buzzing in my ears that would drive a preacher to cuss. Beyond the annoying hum, I can make out a few words of approaching voices. They sound like two ghosts whispering in a graveyard.

"I told you to leave him out of this," one voice says.

"We could not have done it without him. Look how he has

won. Our first major strike against them."

"First major strike?" the first voice says. "We burnt half their research to the ground. What do you—"

"We must hurry. Look at him. If life were a shape, he would not fit the mold."

A man's heavy voice sighs and says, "I'll pack him. It's a long hike to Toadstool. You grab Geiger."

Thudding steps approach above my head. Pressure hits my chest the size of a bear paw. The owner of the hand kneels in front of my face, and a deep, familiar voice coaxes me, "I won't let them bury you too, son."

21

Phorbas' Files | First

C ase File #AG-16
In the Autumn of My 213th Year
Brief: Search for the Beast Speaker.

The following is a recounting of events precisely as memory can serve. Reports of a seeker with an innate ability to conversate with beasts had made its way to my door. Spiraling rumors of life from the other side have always been abundant, but several monsters that strayed beyond our Spikes returned, all telling a similar story.

There was a seeker with a canine android companion and a strip of purple hair that spoke to them. Our known Hyde Foundation informant, the spouse of the lead Hyde Foundation mechanical engineer, has confirmed genome testing to have begun on humans. The lead doctor, Wollston Hyde, is said to have been performing these experiments behind closed doors for decades, but now that his mortality hangs in the balance, he has become bold.

While this does not confirm the existence of one that can

speak to beasts, it does offer a possibility. This doctor, reaching the bottom of sanities pit by the day, coupled with a potential hybrid capable of coercing information from cryptids, is a combination that may indeed bring an end to beast safety. Locating and assessing threat levels is crucial to our survival. Several nights of reconnaissance, following the seeker vehicles to their cryptid-hunting assignments, led to nothing. One night, however, the words of one seeker were not muddled or foreign. This seeker's words were as clear to me as a field of fireflies. From a distance, I watched to confirm my findings against what had been reported by so many others.

I followed their vehicle from above. They traveled north for hours. Around the perimeter of the northern edge of Corinth is a sliver of green. Above that green is a range of mountains. At the foot, the duo of a man and a canine emerged from their transport. The android was plucky in her resolve, and enthusiasm adorned her collar. A scattering, ticking, needle-like sound echoed from her. This sound is from an internal instrument on the beast that allows it to detect radiation — that is how they find us. The seeker is a man. His stature is nothing of note. Perhaps his legend clouded how I might perceive him. The seeker hangs his shoulders low. His disinterest comes across as drowsiness. Do they wake the hybrid only when they have use for his capabilities? Speculation is all we have, even still. I nestled my form into the treetops and never let him escape my curious gaze.

The two of them prattled around the pines for the better of an hour, and the night was at her coldest. Their seeking instrument echoed off bark — any intelligent creature would be avoiding the radius of such a tune. Between the pin-prick noises, I could almost hear their conversations. The man spoke too low in comparison to his fully charged compatriot. If I wanted to hear his voice for myself, I would need to wait for a distraction. My first strike of opportunity was when the prattling reached a peak. Their hunt was close. From my starlight point of view, I watched events unfold as if I was orchestrating them.

The dog slowed its speed and rounded the edge of a wooded brush. This was their first sight of a sasquatch that I had been surveying for some time. Thus far, I was not impressed with the seekers. The sight contact ended the horrid radiation tracker sounds. As the dog returned to his friend, his friend had not stayed where he had last been. Little to either's knowledge, the man had stumbled his way to the far side of the cryptid. Doubling back only separated the partners further from one another. Heavy thuds of fleshy feet pounded their way toward the man. I feared for him. Mere men cannot look thousand-pound behemoths in their beastly eyes and hope to live. This was when the first realization crossed my mind: these seekers very well may need my assistance to survive this encounter.

The man had sense enough to let the beast pass him without being discovered. Not wanting to lose sight or perhaps not feeling the need for his partner, the man pursued the bigfoot's path into the lower hills toward a dugout den. With the dog so naively growing farther away by the moment, I took that time to dare and be closer to the hunt.

As I approached the cave mouth, I heard a voice. It was not the unusually long and exaggerated sounds used when someone is trying to charade their way through understanding with a moth, but clear, plain speech. This seeker was asking the beast intelligent questions. Only once before had a human treated me as an equal.

The man wanted to help the beast; he wanted to return him

home in peace. His pleas with the sasquatch were to no avail, and he quickly became frustrated, but he was trying. One look at the bigfoot, and I knew this was a Hyde Foundation escapee. The monster's eyes were clouded like a midnight storm. Hiders had added something to him or taken something away, but regardless, his guard was up as high as the Spike's reach.

I could not step in and reveal myself yet. The seeker was kind enough to the terrified creature, but he was harsh in his tone and words. Was the seeker trying to de-escalate or taunt the creature? I needed to know this man's true intent before I made an appeal to him. When the sasquatch had enough of the questions and the verbal prodding, he lashed out. A strike from the creature's hand landed on the head of the seeker. As his limp body made a slap on the rocky floor, I stepped in. Not knowing if the boy had just been murdered before my eyes, I felt a responsibility for him. Apathy is colder than death; I would not be apathetic to a mother losing her son.

Before the beast could make another swipe at him, I restrained him. Knowing that he was not in his right mind, I begged for his faculties to return to the forefront. The beast measured me up and down. Recognizing me as a beast like him, and without uttering a word, he hastily evacuated the cave. Alone were I and the seeker. Had he perished, and had I allowed it? His vitals were strong, though his injury seemed severe. Blood painted the floor like his head was melting. Until, suddenly, it stopped. In front of my two eyes, great and curious as they were, the wounds began to close. The hat he wore was flung off his head in the scrap. A stripe, or a patch of purple hair, rested on his crown. Mankind has many colors. The youth of their species often apply dyes to their hair to change its appearance. This hair was not that. This hair reminded me of my kind. Was it so?

Before further study could be conducted, the dog's ticking was approaching. To my amazement, the man had begun to stir back awake. I was forced to retreat to the trees once more. Seeing this seeker up close had restored my hope that the stories were true. The man healed in moments, and he could be understood. If anyone on this side of the wall is capable of surviving the Radlands, it is him. I am certain he will join our fight, just like his father had said he would.

22

Phorbas' Files | Finish

Case File #AG- 20
In the Autumn of My 213th Year
Brief: Scuffle with a Sloth.

The following is a recounting of events precisely as memory can serve. To aid our escape, the responsibility of finishing a formidable foe fell at my true feet. Tensions were high, and Eric was needed elsewhere. Force was used to subdue my enemy combatant — great force. Were he not so large, a lesser force could have been utilized adequately; alas, he was so. If a less violent opportunity had presented itself, I surely would have invited it in to sit a spell.

Moreover, when one such an occurrence did present itself, I welcomed it kindly. Burying leads is no way to fill this log; I digress. From the top, shall we?

From my containment window, I saw every manner of beast. Like columns and rows, stacks of creatures are held behind tempered glass. Many monsters are not reported as missing. We live in nature, and nature has a violent one. It is not uncustomary that a beast be bested by another for the sake of survival. However, for those sentient enough to soak in the sorrow, my finding services can be procured. In this holding lab at the Hyde Foundation, the faces of the reported were scattered all around me.

A bigfoot whose father reported her missing. Her spirit is down, but her time of restraint is up. A gnome whose twin swore they could feel the life of their disappeared sibling. Their eyes are glossed. To none, I can guarantee a safe return, and to none, I can guarantee the one returning is the same one that was lost. But I can, at the maximum minimum, guarantee them their freedom from this prison.

Eric had made his way to this holding lab in disguise. After my coaching, he was able to release my restraints and set my feet back on the path of resolution. The consoles worked exactly as Scott had described. However, the manual release for the cells was not where he said it would be. A search ensued. In the emotions of a mad dash, you would be surprised at how narrow your vision becomes, even with compound eyes. An alarm rang out; someone was activating the sending gate. Eric was many floors up on a walking platform high above me. He began to jump up and down on his head, even as far as standing on CRT-laden desktops, but I could not hear his warning.

There is a feeling, an intuition, that tells us we are being watched or even pursued. A survival instinct that connects every living being. A deer knowing the forest has grown too quiet, a bird sensing it has overstayed its trot on the ground, or a moth realizing the plan has gone a little too perfectly. This feeling brought my shoulders around to face the direction of the door. A hand grabbed me. A large hand. The large arm of the large hand hoisted up to the large height of a large beast. This must be the warden.

Mostly man at his core, like a mega sloth was being pulled out of him the longer his extremities grew. He was, and is, a hulking brute indeed. The poor boy never stood a chance, having been born in this environment. His eyes match his father's. You can practically see the mad scientist brimming from the shape of his brow. His ferocity does not quite match his mother's. He is more brooding than Dr. Fowler. Is it his nature, or perhaps his nurture, or perhaps the lack thereof? Regardless, on that day, the boy chose a fight that he could not win.

While I was reordering my internal priorities, the metal clank of a hundred cells opening in chorus sounded like a symphony to my ears. Unbridled chaos, a stampede of wild beasts being returned to their spirit, the sloth had the *drop* on the moth, as it were, but the herd played quite the distraction. Some freed creatures did not move. They remained perfectly in place. A captor can forget what it means to be free. Freedom is frightful for those who have never known it. Mankind's greatest fear is the unknown, and the present unknown is the degree of torture these prisoners must have endured. What was so great that they could not leave their cage from the frozen fear? I discovered what they were afraid of, at least some of it. Every prisoner fears the fury of a fierce warden.

I flew up, hoping to avoid the rush of beasts. My wings purchased two things for me: freedom from the sloth's clutches and a little bit of time. I tell Eric that this foe is undeserving of the efforts of a combined two moths. Eric is unaware that this hybrid is much like him: lost, young, and unsure he is on the right side of things. Dealing with stubborn young men has become a specialty of mine. It takes some convincing. Being swatted out of the sky through an oak table did me no favors, but Eric finally decides his time is best spent checking in on Dr. Carpenter. As always, the lad must get in a final word. In the midst of his departure, his seeker training takes over. A blinding flash strikes the sloth on his nape, angering and sapping all in one hit. I can't help but smile as I wave Eric off and finally get the chance to show the young bucks what an elder moth's power looks like.

My wings surge me onto the screaming giant. My talons clasp around his lower arms like restraints. The sloth will heal. I take no delight in breaking his two lower arms, but fair is fair, and if I can only use two arms, then so shall it be. His roar echoes up the empty walls when my feet turn his extra set of humeri into gravel. My goal is not to kill him. My goal is to deter him from pursuing me and mine ever again. Perhaps a leg injury will suffice as well.

He swipes his heavy claws at me, but my vision extends further than he knows; I saw the reflexive revenge before he even felt it. His swipe misses, and I punish him with a bite to his shoulder. Again, he instinctively responds and kicks me into the air. I stay there on my wings, waiting to see his next move. His eyes aim at the doors. The fight or flight response within him has shifted. Avoiding the use of his dangling limbs, he forces his weight up and dashes for the exit. My speed in the sky cannot be matched by his on the ground, but again, the young one doesn't know this yet. I fly parallel with him, then outward perpendicular, then toward his legs.

Moths have all manors of gifts. Eric has the stare of penance. My childhood friend, Reuby, can catch wind and fly over speeds of 320 kilometers per hour. And I, Phorbas, have wings with edges sharp as steel. I brush behind the sloth in a near miss, or so he thinks. His heels have been severed from his calves, and crimson drips from the edge of my wing. Down two arms and now two legs, the creature has no fight left in him. Standing over his heaving, breathing chest, hands resting in my pockets, his mother calls out to me from a cell level above.

"What is she saying?" I ask her monstrous son.

"She's pleading for my life. Mom stuff," he replies.

"Assure her I do not intend to claim your life."

Dr. Fowler throws herself on top of her boy, wrapping her arms around his neck.

"She knows, but she's scared," the boy says to me.

"My friends and I are leaving. We couldn't have you blockading our exodus."

Dr. Fowler yells at me for a few moments. Her fangs show, and I'm certain her words are curses.

"Are you closing the portal? We won't be able to leave," he translates.

"The portal will close for good. You're welcome to leave with us, but you must not oppose us."

I turned my back on them. Dr. Fowler called to me, but without her son's interpretation, her cries fell on deaf ears. The last I saw of the hybrid family, the boy was healing and stoic. His mother was frantic and anxious, which permeated the room.

They do not deserve to die. Each of them is the product of an environment that a madman fostered. They played their part in his twisted game, and he has left them to die. Is my leaving them supposed to be any more righteous? Some sort of mercy? I think not. Applying the sins of the father to them is not justice.

But is saving them justice, either? Still, to this day, I am uncertain. When I left them in that room of open cells and trampled floors, they were alive. I did not kill them, but I did not save them either. A moth's true nature, I suppose, exists in the gray. Despite our interference, we will allow things to play out as they may.

Epilogue

Years ago, I had a near heat stroke. Didn't quite advance to that level of severity, but heat exhaustion still feels like an understatement. The heat index was over the century mark, and the last thing on my teenage mind was my H2O consumption. Hell, I just drank when I was thirsty and didn't realize sweet tea and Papa Fizz soda didn't equate to quality water intake.

When your blood has no water in it, it gets thick. That thickness leads to your head feeling light and your body feeling heavy. Your memory gets axed somewhere along the way, too. When your body enters that *keep-me-alive* mode, the order of the queue gets re-stacked. At the top, you have things like breathing, and I suppose at the bottom, you have things like remembering.

One minute, I'm on the floor caking porcelain in yesterday's breakfast. The next, I'm on the couch with a cold, wet towel over my eyes. Finally, I'm in a wheelchair, being stood up and flopped down onto that loud crackling paper that lines a doctor's examination table.

I do remember one thing vividly, though: hating the sight of blood. When the nurse drew my blood, I felt like a tree being sapped. It was the color of dark red wine with the viscosity of honey straight from the hive. Watching that syringe fill made my stomach grab every wall of my rib cage that it could find.

It feels silly to be that close to death, and the solution, pun intended, to bring you back to life is a simple saltwater saline. Not half an hour of being hooked up to an IV and I was feeling back to my old self. The trip to Toadstool was a lot like that.

The part of my brain dedicated to remembering the journey was given a new task, likely something related to stopping the bleeding or keeping me naturally sedated. From the moment Dad picked me up to haul me out of that dirt till about three days ago, I recall nothing. One minute, I'm a winner, victorious over Dr. Hyde. The next, I'm an orphan, and then not an orphan anymore in rather rapid succession. Then, I'm here, with two moths who are not Phorbas rubbing mystery substances on my wounds.

Suffice it to say, waking up in a new place, a village, God knows how far away from the Spikes we entered, was jarring. Geiger was by my side, so I didn't wake up afraid. Phorbas came to check on me shortly after G sprinted out of my room screaming so loud I thought her speakers would burst.

Phorbas stops by at least twice a day to visit my bedridden body. Geiger hardly ever leaves me. She says the little mothmen, the mothchildren, I guess, pull her tail like it's a game, and she doesn't much care for it. I guess my hollowed-out, overgrown mushroom tree house doubles as her hiding place.

Dad tried coming by a few times. Eventually, he understood that my silence was voluntary. I've got nothing to say to him. Not yet. All those years, I talked at the moon to his ghost. Here I am now with him right in front of me, and I can't say a word. Phorbas has been preaching to me about forgiveness. The way I see it, he's lucky I forgive him for not telling me that his mystery friend was my dead dad this whole time.

How close I truly came to death is not exactly a calculable statistic. She didn't claim me, that seductive mistress, but it took some time to fully swat her sweet nothings away from their nibble on my earlobe. My healing was slower than ever. Granted, my injuries were far more severe than ever. Every morning and every night, two moth healers check on me. Their medicines smell like shit, and they won't tell me what's in them, so it's likely shit.

Geiger was in need of a few minor repairs. Like the town of Kelly, whoever repaired her had to make do with what they had. Her once pristine white plastic and carbon steel frame is now a bit dingy in spots and rusty in others. I think this look fits her better if I'm honest.

This town of Toadstool apparently has quite a bit of hand-me-down technology. I haven't gotten out of my bed yet; the healers think I should stay down for a while, but I know they at least have radio communication here.

A transmission came through. It was choppy, definitely at the far reaches of our antenna range, but the sentiment of the message was clear.

Maybe trying to goad me into breaking my silent treatment, Dad came in and told me that he heard Mom in that transmission; he knew it was her. They couldn't make contact and reach back out, but it was her.

The queen of tech had performed yet another miracle. Somehow, some way, the implosion of the teleporter didn't kill her. Phorbas theorizes that she directed the energy to another link. The cascading energies needed a release, and the only way to do that was to make a jump, taking the teleporter and anything caught in the blast radius with it.

In order for the teleporter to go somewhere else, that implies it had another receiver to go to. How many tunnels through time and space did Hyde have? At least one more, we now know.

When I heal, when these moths stop rubbing medicinal mud and herbs on my wings, we are setting out. Our course is a treacherous one, according to the rough triangulation of the transmission signal. If we are right, we have a lot of preparation to do before we brave the great gray fog that hovers over the incredible Glowing Sea.

I don't care what it takes. We heard you, Mom. We're coming. And I dare anything to try and stop us.

About the Author

Seth Patrick is an American novelist raised in the sticks of Western Kentucky. Writing as a hobbyist, Seth works by day in software quality assurance. After hours, he can be found clearing a Netflix library or an Xbox backlog. Never short on ideas of the odd, the sci-fi, the fantasy, or the horror, he always has a notebook in his hand and caffeine in his brain. He lives alone but close to home, close to the lake, and close to church. This is his first-ever novel.

Made in the USA
Monee, IL
06 May 2025